THE DERBY DAREDEVILS

TOMOKO TAKES THE LEAD

BREE

Shelly

Tomoko

Kenzie

Jules

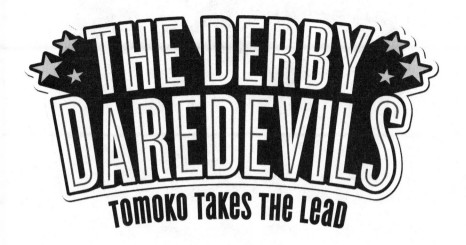

THE DERBY DAREDEVILS

TOMOKO TAKES THE LEAD

BY KIT ROSEWATER

ILLUSTRATED BY
SOPHIE ESCABASSE

AMULET BOOKS
NEW YORK

Cataloging-in-Publication Data has been applied for and may be obtained from the Library of Congress.

ISBN 978-1-4197-5172-1

Text copyright © 2021 Christyl Rosewater
Illustrations copyright © 2021 Sophie Escabasse
Book design by Marcie Lawrence

Published in 2021 by Amulet Books, an imprint of ABRAMS. All rights reserved.
No portion of this book may be reproduced, stored in a retrieval system, or transmitted in any form or by any means, mechanical, electronic, photocopying, recording, or otherwise, without written permission from the publisher.

Printed and bound in U.S.A.
10 9 8 7 6 5 4 3 2 1

Amulet Books are available at special discounts when purchased in quantity for premiums and promotions as well as fundraising or educational use. Special editions can also be created to specification. For details, contact specialsales@abramsbooks.com or the address below.

Amulet Books® is a registered trademark of Harry N. Abrams, Inc.

ABRAMS The Art of Books
195 Broadway, New York, NY 10007
abramsbooks.com

For Jim, who taught me when to follow the signs
and when to blaze the trail.
Thank you, Dad.
–K.R.

CHAPTER ONE

THE WARM AUSTIN AIR SIZZLED OVER THE CONCRETE AS beats pulsed from someone's cell phone.

Boom-che, boom-che, boom-che, boom-che.

Tomoko bounced her basketball in rhythm, lifting and pressing the ball down and down and down like a baker kneading dough.

"Are you sure this is going to work?" Shelly called from the other end of the court.

Tomoko looked up and smiled. She tightened the helmet strap under her chin.

"No," she said. "That's why we're trying it!"

Tomoko's teammates were spread out over the basketball court at the park. Shelly stood near the hoop in the small forward position, Kenzie and Bree took center positions halfway down the court, and Jules stood as point guard, just across from Tomoko.

If the five girls were wearing sneakers and long shorts, they might have looked exactly like a basketball team. And they did make up a team—they had been the Daredevils ever since the spring. Instead of basketball gear, the Daredevils were decked out in skates, elbow and knee pads, wrist guards, and helmets. They were one of the toughest roller derby teams in the Austin league, but today derby practice was taking place somewhere new.

"What if basketball and derby don't go together as well as you think?" Kenzie asked.

Tomoko stopped dribbling. She tucked the ball under her arm. "Oh come on. It's fun to try things together! We can help each other learn how to play basketball on wheels."

That was easy for Tomoko to say, of course. She knew she wouldn't need any help out on the court. She could trade in her sneakers for skates and still weave the ball between her legs. That was one of the reasons Tomoko loved basketball. She had been shooting hoops for so long, now she could sink baskets with her eyes closed.

But Tomoko also loved being around her team. In that way, basketball and derby went together perfectly.

"And, go!" Tomoko said. She slid one skate forward, dribbling the ball next to her. Jules lunged for the ball. She nearly wiped out on her skates, the way she used to when they first started the Daredevils team months ago. But this time, Jules caught her balance. She clawed at the air and swiped for Tomoko again.

"Hi-yah!" Jules cried. "Shoot! I keep missing it!"

Tomoko turned on her skates and dribbled down the center of the court. Bree dove for Tomoko, ready to deliver a firm hip check. But Tomoko twisted again, the ball thumping against her palm.

"Shelly!" Kenzie cried. "Go for it!"

Shelly waved her hands in the air like a chicken trying to take flight. Tomoko cocked the ball back.

"She's too tall!" Shelly said.

Swoosh!

The basketball sank cleanly into the net.

Shelly whistled as she watched the ball bounce back onto the pavement. "Nice one, Tomonater!"

"I want to be on Tomoko's team this time," Jules said. "Two against three!"

"She already beats us one against four," Kenzie said. She put her hand on her hip. "The point of the game is to make it interesting."

Bree skated over to Tomoko and knocked her elbow playfully. "We'll get better over the summer," she said. "And by the time school starts again, I'll bet we could make Tomoko work a little harder for all those shots!"

Tomoko grinned and nudged Bree back. She imagined the orange juice–colored skies of Austin's summertime, when the evenings stretched on forever and she stayed at the park for hours. Last summer, Tomoko had spent all those park hours by herself. She could shoot hoops on her

own all day, but it was so much nicer to have a team around her. The boys who played pickup games at the park could be mean, and no one used to stand up for Tomoko when they kicked her off the court. But everything was different now that the Daredevils had banded together. Now Tomoko always had a team to play on—even when she wanted to make up silly games like roller derby basketball!

"I think I'm beat for the day," Kenzie said. She unclipped her helmet and shook out her hair. "Come on. If we return the gear now, we'll have time for ice pops before I have to go home!"

Jules stuck out her tongue. "I don't feel like ice pops," she said. "How about some pizza?"

"I want fried avocado tacos!" Shelly said. She licked her lips.

Tomoko shrugged. She would be happy anywhere hanging out with her friends.

"Let's hit up the Juicy World stand," Bree said. "They have like every type of juice, and fries and stuff too. We can all get something different."

The team nodded and gathered their backpacks on the edge of the court. They skated single file down the sidewalk, bumping over the uneven panels of pavement.

Tomoko's knees vibrated as her wheels slid over textured drain covers. She tucked her basketball by her side and looked out at all her favorite shops and murals along South Congress Avenue. She passed by a pale green wall with a love letter swirled over it in red paint. She waved to the man who ran the pizza place and always gave Tomoko extra pineapple when she ordered her ham and pineapple slice.

Next time, I hope we get pizza, Tomoko thought as the girls rounded the corner.

Tomoko dipped under the awning of a tea shop that had the best hot chocolate in the winter. She passed by a wall that said *Greetings from Austin* with pictures of all her favorite buildings from downtown. The colors and smells whirled together in Tomoko's head as the team made the usual trip from the park to the derby warehouse.

The first time they had turned some of the corners onto new streets, Tomoko felt like she was lost in a giant maze of buildings. But now every doorway and front porch seemed familiar. Tomoko loved feeling like the city belonged to her.

"Only one more week of having to wear this dumb thing," Jules said as she pulled her backpack straps tighter.

All the elbow pads, knee pads, wrist guards, and helmets were back in the derby box at the warehouse. All the rental skates were lined up on the counter. The Daredevils slid out the front doors in normal tennis shoes, like superheroes pretending to be their alter egos.

Shelly adjusted her backpack. "I can't wait until school's done," she said.

"Yeah," Jules said. "Then we can dump all the vocabulary lists and math tests from our brains and let everything drain right out!"

"Learning is a lifelong endeavor," Bree said.

Tomoko looked over her shoulder. "What does that mean?"

Bree shrugged. "My dad says it a lot. I think he just means you never stop learning, even when you're not in school."

"That makes sense." Kenzie shoved her own skates

into her backpack. "We'll be learning new derby moves all summer with the league."

Jules grinned. "Derby is way more my type of learning," she said. "We'll be filling up our feet and hips with derby know-how, not our brains!"

Shelly laughed and nodded. "Derby's my type of learning too. Well, that and art class."

"I know I'm sure ready for summer," Kenzie said.

"Me too," Bree said.

Bree and Kenzie smiled at each other. Tomoko knew that the two of them were happy about the summer for two reasons. The first great thing about summer was the regular stuff Jules was talking about, like throwing old homework away and getting to practice derby whenever they wanted.

But Tomoko could tell that they were happy for a second, secret reason. Since Bree went to a different school than the rest of the Daredevils, they only got to see her after class and on weekends. Soon they'd have whole days to themselves for skating around and playing at the park. Everyone missed Bree during the school day, but especially Kenzie. Bree and Kenzie liked each other. Tomoko found out about their crush right when the team was getting started.

Kenzie and Bree had their own secrets, but what neither of them knew—what none of the other Daredevils knew—was that Tomoko also had a second, secret reason for being excited for the summer.

Math quizzes and history papers were no fun, but for Tomoko, school was a lot harder than just doing work. Before Shelly and Kenzie invited Tomoko onto the team, school mostly meant Tomoko avoiding everybody. Sometimes kids teased Tomoko about her size or about the food she brought for lunch whenever her mom packed delicious leftover yakisoba.

Kenzie and Shelly never had to worry about not having friends. They always had each other. But, for Tomoko, being on the Daredevils was like having a super amazing circle of protection wherever she went.

And now that they were about to have three whole months away from school and all the cold looks and mean comments, Tomoko was ready for the best Austin summer ever. She couldn't wait to see what adventures the Daredevils would go on next.

CHAPTER TWO

WHOOSH!

The cold shower water splashed down over Tomoko. She stood in her bathing suit under the nozzle and counted to ten, then switched the faucet off and peeked over her stall. The outdoor shower area at Barton Springs was packed with people, but Tomoko didn't recognize any of the faces.

"Kenzie? Shelly?"

Tomoko nudged the door open. She grabbed her towel and held it slightly in front of her, not wanting to get it wet before she even had a chance to jump in the pool.

"Hello? Jules? Bree?"

The chatter and bustle of bodies made Tomoko's stomach tighten with nervousness. She stepped out of the stall and through the narrow aisle of people. Mostly everyone

was focused on grabbing their swimsuits from their lockers or finding their bottles of sunscreen, but Tomoko could still feel a few eyes slip over to her. She always felt stares, the same way a person could feel an icy chill over their skin. Tomoko hated being in her swimsuit alone. She shivered and made her way out to the pool.

The rest of the Daredevils had their towels piled up along the grassy hill. Bree and Kenzie were practicing underwater headstands while Jules and Shelly swam the width of the pool, back and forth.

Tomoko dropped her towel on the pile and folded her arms tight in front of her chest.

"Heya, Tomonater!" Jules called. "Come on in! The water's nice and icy cold!"

"It's not icy cold," Shelly said. She cupped a handful of water as if she were testing it. "It's just not that warm. But you get used to it!"

Tomoko only frowned.

"How come you all left me?" she asked.

Jules swam to the edge of the pool. "You took forever to put on your swimsuit! You saw how crowded it was in the locker room. It felt weird to just be standing there."

Tomoko sighed. Jules was right. Still, she didn't like being left alone, especially in new places where she didn't know anyone. She hadn't been to Barton Springs since last summer, and even then, she only went with her uncle, who always pretended like the Loch Ness monster was grabbing him and made everyone give them strange looks.

She shook the memory from her head and held on to the rungs of the ladder. Her feet plunged into the water. Bree and Kenzie twisted out of their headstands.

"Ooh, it is cold," Tomoko said.

"Not for long," Bree said. "Plus, you can see tons of plants at the bottom once you dunk your head. It's awesome!"

Tomoko smiled, then pushed herself from the side and held her breath as she swam under the surface with her friends.

She popped her eyes open one at a time. *Pop! Pop!* Far below, long emerald-green leaves rippled in the current like flags. Tiny fish threaded through the leaves, swimming with the water as it passed through the springs and on to the river. Tomoko could almost imagine a Loch Ness monster swimming with them.

The Daredevils spent all afternoon at the springs. They had ice pops and sandwiches for lunch, then dried off in the sun and found funky shapes in the clouds. Then they raced by rolling down the grass hill.

"I bet we could work this into derby somehow," Kenzie said.

"Nuh-uh." Bree shook her head. "I am *not* wearing skates in the water."

Kenzie laughed. "I mean like the hill races. We should come up here every weekend and practice rolling around so we can move out of the way when we fall on the track."

Tomoko nodded. She glanced around at the springs. She could get used to coming up here every weekend, especially with the Daredevils.

The next morning, Tomoko got to go to one of her favorite places—one she was already used to. She zipped up her roller derby bag and made her way downstairs for breakfast.

"Morning," Tomoko's mom said. She turned from the counter holding two plates of omelets. She set one plate in front of Tomoko's uncle Randall and the other in front an open seat waiting for Tomoko.

"Ohayō," Randall said.

"Good morning, ojichan," Tomoko said.

Randall set the book he was reading down by his side and picked up a fork. Tomoko glanced at the book's cover as

she picked up her own fork. It was a field guide on birds in South Texas.

"Idatakimasu! Dig in," Randall said.

"Idatakimasu," Tomoko echoed. She sliced her fork sideways into her omelet. "Getting ready for another big camping trip this summer?"

"Of course," Randall said. "Just like always." He glanced up from his plate. "Aren't you going to be there too?"

Tomoko shook her head. "Not this year. I'm really busy with roller derby practices and the team. The coaches are doing a summer program for the league."

Her uncle furrowed his brow. "No Tomochan out on the trails this year?"

Tomoko's mom sat down at the table. "Come now, ane," she said. "We all knew Tomoko would get tired of the trails eventually."

She turned to Tomoko and brushed a piece of Tomoko's hair behind her ear. "I think roller derby has been really wonderful for you. I'm so happy to see you so busy with new friends."

Tomoko blushed. "They're old friends now." She wolfed the last of her omelet down. "So good. Domo, okaachan," she said to her mom.

"So ne," Randall added. "Breakfast was delicious."

Tomoko's mom smiled and nodded. She began gathering plates.

Tomoko grabbed her bag. "Be home later!"

"Bye, honey!" her mom called.

Randall picked up his bird guide again.

Tomoko thought about the bird on the guide's cover as she walked the several blocks to the derby warehouse. It was a green jay, a bird with a cobalt-blue head and bright green body. She remembered first seeing that bird out with her uncle years ago on one of their camping trips. At the time, Tomoko felt like the coolest kid in the world. But now those camping trips with her uncle seemed so dorky. She never even found one person her age to hang with at the campgrounds.

A bird cried out overhead. Tomoko peeked up into the branches, but just like she thought—it wasn't a rare bird at all. Just the grackle, a blackbird that hung out all over Austin and wailed like a siren. She hurried along the rest of the way to the warehouse.

Ffftt!

Mambo Rambo spit out the whistle in her mouth. "Jammer line!" she called.

The five Austin junior league roller derby teams gathered

and took a knee. Tomoko was sandwiched between Bree and Shelly. All the girls were sweaty and smelly from a full morning of practice.

"Well done," Razzle Dazzle said, standing next to Mambo and their third coach, Look Out. "Y'all have made it through the spring season of roller derby!"

Everyone in the league cheered. Tomoko grinned and clapped her hands.

"I wonder if you can guess what's coming next," Lo said.

"Summer season!" Tomoko chanted along with the other players. They all laughed and cheered again.

The coaches laughed too. "That's right," Raz said. "We're checking off the spring and moving on to summer!"

Mambo cleared her throat. "Since this is our first year running the league, we're still figuring out program activities. But luckily, roller derby is all about teamwork, and that includes teamwork between the coaches. Our nearby Dallas league has agreed to team up with us in planning the perfect summer of derby fun."

Tomoko liked the sound of the perfect summer of derby fun. But what did Mambo mean when she said they were teaming up with the Dallas coaches? Hopefully things wouldn't be too different from their normal practices. That was already a perfect summer of fun for Tomoko.

"Dallas has been running their summer derby program for three years now, and it's a well-oiled machine," Mambo went on. "So we've decided to hop on their bandwagon. This year we'll be helping to put on a sleepaway summer derby camp!"

"Sleepaway camp?" someone said.

Two girls squealed over Tomoko's shoulder. She turned and caught Jules's eye, who gave her a big thumbs-up. Tomoko gave a thumbs-up back to Jules, but she was still confused. She looked around the warehouse. Where would they be sleeping? Were the girls supposed to bring sleeping bags and cots to the track?

"But we're not having the camp here . . ." Lo said.

Even though the three coaches were smiling, Tomoko's

heart flopped over sideways. They were going somewhere *new*? Just as summer was getting started?

She took a breath and squeezed her hands tight.

The rest of the junior league players had leaned forward, waiting for Lo to tell them where they were going.

"We'll be holding summer camp in Dallas with their junior league!" Lo said. "So get ready to see new things, try new moves, and make some new friends!"

Anyone sitting in the bleachers would have thought the derby players were just told they were each getting brand-new skates and free passes to the snack bar for life with the yelling and excitement that went up around the warehouse.

But there was one voice that did not whoop along with the others.

New things?

New moves?

New friends?

Tomoko picked at one of her nails, trying to look busy so she wouldn't have to turn and grin at her teammates like everyone else. This summer was supposed to be about spending time with her group, in all the places she loved.

What would it be like, she wondered, to have to spend it somewhere entirely new?

CHAPTER THREE

"FREEDOM!" JULES CRIED OUT AS SHE RAN TO THE park.

Tomoko, Kenzie, and Shelly were behind her. Each of them carried a limp backpack. Lockers and cubbies had been cleared out. Classroom books had been turned in. The dangling loose straps over their shoulders meant it was finally time for summer.

But Jules's pack still sagged and smacked against her back as she ran. While Tomoko saw most of the kids at Curie Elementary empty out their folders and notebooks into the recycling bins at school, Jules insisted on keeping all her papers together.

"For now," she had told Tomoko while wagging her eyebrows mischievously.

Tomoko saw exactly what that meant as she watched Jules run across the park field and over to the blue recycling bin next to the playground. Jules unzipped her bag with a flourish and held it over her head with both hands.

"As Crown Jules, I royally declare the school year over!"

"Hear, hear, Your Highness!" Bree curled around the park corner on her skateboard, her own backpack also stuffed full. She bounced off her board and ran to the recycling bin across from Jules.

"You too?" Kenzie asked.

Bree and Jules grinned at the other Daredevils.

"I'm all for lifelong learning," Bree said. "But that doesn't mean I don't love a good royal backpack dumping!"

She turned her bag upside down along with Jules. A cascade of scribbled notebook pages tumbled into the bin.

Kenzie, Shelly, and Tomoko laughed as the papers rained down. Once both bags were empty, Bree and Jules tossed them onto the grass like empty corn husks. The Daredevils spread out over the field, making summer snow angels and wiggling around in the perfect feeling of having nothing to do and all the free time they wanted.

"Should we do an off-skates workout today?" Kenzie asked finally.

Tomoko propped herself up on one elbow. "I could go for that."

"Nah," Shelly said. "We have a bajillion days to practice now. We can work on our signature Daredevils moves whenever."

"That's not true." Bree sat up and brushed the grass from her sleeves. "You heard what Lo said at practice last weekend. We'll be heading off to derby camp soon!"

Jules rolled over the grass until she bumped into Bree's side.

"Derby camp!" she shouted. "I can't wait!"

"What kinds of things do you think we'll do there?" Shelly asked.

"Hip check each other and eat a lot of s'mores, probably," Jules said.

Bree smiled. "Maybe it will be like a boot camp for derby players," she said. She stood up and leaped onto their meeting rock. "Maybe we'll have to lift boulders and balance on branches and jump over rivers!"

Kenzie got up after Bree. "And maybe at night we'll sit around the campfire and tell ghost stories about old roller derby players."

"I don't think roller derby's *that* old," Bree said.

Kenzie shrugged. "Well, my mom plays it. So."

"I hope there are toilets," Shelly said. "The kind that flush—not big holes in the ground full of poop. Bleh. Gross."

"I just hope there's an outdoor track," Jules said. "What good is roller derby camp if you can't roll around anywhere?"

Shelly nudged Tomoko's side. "What are you hoping for?" she asked.

Tomoko stared into the grass.

I'm hoping to stay right here, she thought. But she didn't want to ruin everyone else's fun.

Tomoko shrugged. "Anything's OK, I guess."

Kenzie laughed. "You always say that," she said. "You never pick anything out."

"Oh," Tomoko said. She had never thought about it that way before. She liked having a group of friends wherever she went. Technically, Tomoko felt like she was picking something all the time. She always picked being with friends over being lonely.

"I think derby camp will be great no matter what," Bree said. "It's camp and roller derby! Where can you go wrong? Hey, Tomoko, do you have your basketball? Maybe we can shoot a few hoops since we're not practicing today."

Tomoko shook her head. She had left her ball at home so she wouldn't lose it in all the chaos of the last day of school.

"That's OK," Kenzie said. "Maybe we can play a game instead."

"Like what?" Shelly asked.

Kenzie grinned. "Anyone up for freeze tag?"

Bree jumped down from the rock. "Not it!"

"Not it!" the other Daredevils echoed, scrambling to their feet.

"Guess that leaves me, then," Kenzie said. "Kenzilla is going to get you all!"

She roared and took off across the field.

Tomoko laughed and ran around in zigzags as Kenzie chased them down. Then she ran as Crown Jules hurtled through the park. Jules tagged Tomoko, and the Tomonater stomped every which way until she tagged Shelly. The girls

had been playing for over half an hour before Bomb Shell finally landed an explosive tag on Bree.

"Oh, y'all better watch out now!" Bree yelled.

The Daredevils all jetted across the field, but Bree was known as Bree Zee for a reason. In less than a minute she tagged Kenzie by the rock.

"You were only 'it' for two seconds!" Kenzie cried.

"Quit moaning and be happy I'm on your team as jammer," Bree said.

Both Kenzie and Bree laughed. Bree hip checked into Kenzie's side and Kenzie hip checked her right back. Tomoko could tell that the game of freeze tag was over and the game of Kenzie and Bree clowning around was starting.

She walked back to the meeting rock with Shelly and Jules. Tomoko looked across at the swings creaking and the kids laughing as they rolled around in the sandbox. She would miss this. Why couldn't they be spending the whole summer here like they planned?

"Think about how much fun freeze tag will be in the woods!" Jules said. "We'll have to duck around big trees while we outrun each other."

Tomoko mustered a small smile.

"I like playing freeze tag here," she said quietly.

Shelly turned over her shoulder to Tomoko. Shelly

sometimes had a way of looking at Tomoko that showed she could hear the things Tomoko was saying *and* the things Tomoko was thinking. That was part of what made her such a good friend.

"You're still going to derby camp, though," Shelly said. She paused. "Right?"

Tomoko shrugged. "I don't want to be here alone."

Kenzie and Bree stopped goofing off. Everyone gathered in a classic Daredevils huddle around Tomoko.

"Why would you be here alone?" Bree said. "I thought we were all going together."

"Well . . ." Tomoko rubbed her arm. "I'm not sure."

"What aren't you sure about?" Kenzie asked.

Tomoko looked at her teammates. She could feel the warmth creeping into her face. "It's just . . . that's a lot of new people."

Shelly cocked her head. "You mean the kids from Dallas? I'll bet they're just like the roller derby players here. Plus, remember how cool the teams from New Mexico were in the spring tournament? You get along so well with everyone, Tomonater!"

When they're nice to me, Tomoko thought.

"You gotta come to camp," Jules said. "It won't be any fun without you."

That made Tomoko smile. She liked everyone wanting her to be around.

"I'll . . . try," she said gently.

"That's the spirit!" Jules clapped Tomoko on the back. "The Daredevils are in this together! We're an unstoppable force of nature! Watch out!"

Jules flung her arms out to the side and spun around the field in circles. Shelly leaned in to Tomoko.

"Sometimes I think Jules wishes we would have been the Dust Devils instead of the Daredevils."

Tomoko laughed alongside Shelly.

She wanted derby camp to be as fun as regular Daredevils practices. And maybe it would be. The skaters from the junior Albuquerque league were all nice at the tournament Austin held a couple months before. But still, Tomoko had learned from lots of other experiences that people weren't always nice right off the bat.

Tomoko looked around at her teammates. She hoped they would find a way to have fun in Dallas . . . even if that meant bunking with a bunch of new players.

CHAPTER FOUR

TOMOKO SLIPPED BACK THROUGH HER FRONT DOOR later that evening. She let her empty backpack flop onto the coat hook and stepped into the kitchen.

Uncle Randall was in his usual chair, this time reading a guidebook about South Texas reptiles and amphibians. The guide had an indigo snake on the front.

"Meikko," Randall said, looking over the book. "How was school?"

"Over," Tomoko said. She gave a half smile. "My backpack is empty."

"Your smile's pretty empty too," Randall said. He pulled out the chair next to him and patted the seat.

Tomoko shuffled over to the chair and slumped in.

"Tell me what's going on," her uncle said. He set the guide down to show he was really listening.

Tomoko sighed. "Roller derby is doing a summer camp."

"So you told us," Randall said.

"No." Tomoko shook her head. "I thought we were just having a summer season. But we found out they're doing a sleepaway camp with the Dallas derby league. The rest of the Daredevils are going, and they say I have to go too."

Her uncle Randall raised an eyebrow.

"You don't want to go?" he asked.

"No, I do," Tomoko said. "Well, I think I do. I want to be with my team. And I really don't want to spend the summer alone. There will just be so many new people at camp. I don't know what they'll be like."

Randall eyed Tomoko for a moment. He pushed his chair back from the table and turned for the front door.

"Let's go for a walk," he said. He grabbed his pair of binoculars from the coat rack. "I've been meaning to watch the bats come out at dusk. You interested?"

Sometimes Tomoko worried about the looks people would give her when she was out with her uncle while he wore his khaki shorts and shirt and floppy hat. It didn't help that he had his binoculars pressed to his eyes and pointed and shouted up at the branches in the middle of downtown.

But she did love watching the bats stream out of the South Congress Bridge.

"Sure," Tomoko said. She followed her uncle out of the house and down the sidewalk toward Lady Bird Lake.

They waded through the throng of shoppers along South Congress. Tomoko didn't like how busy the shops could be in the evenings. People tended to be grumpier at that time in the day, frowning whenever they all had to squeeze together to cross a street or wait their turn and walk right behind someone else. Shopping bags brushed and bumped against Tomoko's side. Jules always complained about how hard it was being short in crowds, but it wasn't so easy being bigger or taller either.

Sometimes Tomoko wanted to hip check everyone out of the way, but most of the time she just wanted to disappear.

The rush of shoppers finally thinned as Tomoko and Randall emerged closer to the water, where a whole different crowd was forming over the bridge. A lot of people were holding binoculars, just like her uncle.

"Come on," Randall said. He grinned and swiveled off the main road. Tomoko turned after him, staring at her feet as the slate pavement turned into a dirt trail.

They crept into the trees, sliding under the canopy where far fewer people were standing. The trees made Tomoko feel a little more at home. She followed her uncle to a flat rock jutting up against the water. They climbed onto the rock and sat cross-legged. The onlookers at the bridge leaned forward. Everyone was waiting for the sun to slip a little farther in the sky, for the evening to draw out the bats that lived under the bridge.

Randall slid the binoculars off his neck and handed them to Tomoko.

"See any movement?"

Tomoko aimed the binoculars toward the bridge. Every now and then, a pair of black wings fluttered out from under the arch. The bats came to the South Congress Bridge every summer to huddle tightly between the concrete beams. The space was wide enough for them to get in, but narrow enough to keep all their predators out. Tomoko thought it was smart the way the bats made sure to stay protected.

"A little movement," Tomoko said. "I think they're getting ready."

As if her voice had lowered an invisible gate, suddenly a loud *whirr*ing sound came from the bridge. The first group

of bats took off from the beams, rising into the air and speckling the soft, pale sky.

"They're here!" Randall said.

Tomoko watched the group funnel farther toward the east, unspooling into a line soaring over the water. She handed the binoculars back to her uncle. He studied the bridge as the next group of bats left their homes to hunt for mosquitos.

"Do you know what they call a group of bats?" he asked.

Tomoko scrunched her forehead. "A colony, I think?"

Randall nodded. "Sometimes. But they're also known as a camp of bats."

Tomoko arched an eyebrow. "Is that why you brought me here?"

"Of course not," her uncle said. "I always want to see the bats."

He looked away from his binoculars over to Tomoko and smiled. "OK, maybe it was a little bit of the reason. A camp of bats! That's a pretty neat coincidence, right?"

Tomoko smiled. "I guess so."

"The main reason I wanted you to come out with me is to talk," Randall said. "I want to know why you're afraid of meeting new people."

Tomoko's cheeks turned pink at the corners. "I'm not afraid exactly."

"Then what is it?" Randall asked. "Why are you nervous about camp?"

The pink in her cheeks wouldn't go away. How could Tomoko explain how other people treated her without seeming like a total loser?

"I guess . . . sometimes I get nervous that other people will push me away. Or not give me a chance in the first place. Because of my size or other things about me."

She waited for her uncle to ask more questions. But when she turned to him, he didn't seem confused. Randall looked like he knew exactly what Tomoko was talking about.

"I understand that," he said softly.

Even though it wasn't cold outside at all, Tomoko hugged herself around her waist. She couldn't decide if she was happy that her uncle knew exactly what she was talking about, or sad that he must've felt that way too at some point.

"Derby's different," Tomoko said hopefully. "At least here it's different. When my friends are around, everything's great. I get to be myself and relax and have fun."

"But you're worried the kids in Dallas might not be the same way."

Tomoko nodded.

Randall sighed through his nose, threading the binoculars

around his neck again. The last camp of bats was sailing into the horizon.

"Let's grab something to eat on the way home," he said. He led Tomoko back along the trail and onto the sidewalk.

The crowds over the bridge clustered off, turning toward their cars. Shops along South Congress were flipping their signs from *Come in for good times* to *You blew it, we're closed.* Tomoko pointed to the pizza place the Daredevils had skated past last week.

"Can we go here?"

Randall pressed the binoculars to his eyes and stared at the sign a few feet way.

"Looks like they're open!" he said cheerily.

Tomoko smiled, though her cheeks flushed as she caught a few stares from other people.

Randall held the door for Tomoko. He tapped his fingers on the binoculars as they waited in line.

"You know, meikko," he said, "this could be a wonderful opportunity for you."

"What?" Tomoko asked. "Pineapple pizza?"

"Well, of course pineapple pizza," Randall said. "But I mean the summer camp. I'll bet a lot of these girls haven't been camping before."

Tomoko thought of what Shelly said at the park about

being afraid of going to the bathroom in outhouses or in the woods.

"That's true," she said.

"But you're a natural camper. Been out every year with me since you were little."

"Uh-huh."

Randall splayed his hands wide. "This means you'll have tons of opportunity to get along with everyone! You can be like a troop leader out there!"

Tomoko squinted at her uncle. She couldn't remember being the leader of anything ever, except maybe a few Daredevils plays where she directed the blocking moves. But then again, he had a point. Tomoko knew her way around on skates *and* in hiking boots. She was sort of like an expert in both.

Tomoko thought about what it would be like to be proud and confident at camp. She pictured herself fist-bumping and high-fiving everyone along the trails. A slow grin spread across her face.

"Now *that's* a full smile," Randall said. He ruffled Tomoko's hair and stepped to the counter to order.

CHAPTER FIVE

THE AUSTIN SUMMER SUN FLOODED TOMOKO'S ROOM as she stood with her hands on her hips. Her empty hiking backpack was propped against her bedside. The roller derby camp packing list sat on the bed. Tomoko picked up the list and scanned it over again.

"Hmmm," she said aloud.

The list had normal enough stuff for camping. It included all the sets of clothes they'd need for a week away from home. It made sure the players all brought their bathroom bags with soap and toothpaste and toothbrushes.

"And a towel," Tomoko read. She frowned. The list didn't say to pack a swimsuit, but usually the only way to get clean while camping was dipping into a lake or river. Maybe the coaches just forgot to add *swimsuit* to the list.

Tomoko grabbed her swimsuit from her dresser and a towel from the hall closet. She threw them on the bed.

She pulled out shorts and leggings and long socks. She pulled out sunscreen and bug spray. She even pulled out her hiking books and her own, smaller set of binoculars—even though the list forgot those things too. Like Uncle Randall had said: Maybe this was Tomoko's big chance to be a leader in the group. She would need to be prepared to make sure everyone would see her as the leader type.

Soon, every bit of Tomoko's hiking backpack was stuffed full of supplies. She slid water bottles into the outer pockets, along with a compass and some extra bandages. She rolled all her clothes into tight little balls and placed them neatly along the bottom of the main pocket.

Tomoko was just pulling the drawstring at the top of the bag closed when her mom knocked gently along the doorframe.

"You're doing a pretty good job with packing," she said.

Tomoko looked over her shoulder and smiled. "The list forgot a bunch of stuff. Good thing I already know how to camp. I have to help all the other Daredevils. Shelly's even afraid to pee in the woods!"

Her mom laughed. She drew something from behind her back. It was Tomoko's basketball.

"Any room for this?"

Tomoko stood up from her bag and took the ball gingerly from her mom's hands.

"I don't think it will fit in the pack," Tomoko said. She wedged the ball under her arm. "But I can carry it on the bus. You never know when you might need a basketball!"

She hugged her mom and set the ball beside her bag. As Tomoko looked the bundle over, she swelled with confidence. Camping, roller derby, and basketball—the three things she was best at. She had to make friends at a camp with all three of those things. She just had to.

Tomoko's mom and uncle dropped her off outside the derby warehouse the next day. Kenzie was already standing by the front doors with her mom. She had her regular roller derby duffel flung over her shoulder, then a second duffel bag by her side.

"I didn't want all my regular clothes to get smelly," Kenzie explained.

Tomoko nodded. She twisted her shoulders to set her hiking pack down.

"Whoa," Kenzie said. "Did you fit everything in there?"

"Oh yeah," Tomoko said. "Even more stuff than they had on the list. They actually forgot a lot."

Kenzie wrinkled her forehead. "Really?"

"Don't worry," Tomoko said. "We'll all be fine. I brought extra wool socks to share if you need some."

"Thanks," Kenzie said. "I didn't bring *any* wool socks."

Shelly showed up with her mom, then Bree, then Jules. All the other Daredevils only had duffel bags. Tomoko looked around as the rest of the league approached the front doors with their families. No one brought a hiking

pack but her. Was she really the only one in the whole league who went camping?

For a moment, Tomoko wanted to fold in on herself. She hunched her shoulders, trying to hide the giant backpack leaning against her shins. But then she remembered what Randall had said at the pizza place. This was Tomoko's big chance to be a leader. She puffed out her chest and clutched tightly to one of the backpack straps.

Mambo Rambo and Look Out emerged through the front doors. Mambo was carrying a clipboard.

"All right, league!" she called out. "Are you ready for Dallas?"

"Yeah!" all the players cheered. This time Tomoko made sure to cheer along.

"Where's Raz?" Bree asked.

Beep beep!

Bree's question was answered as a green school bus cruised down the road. Raz honked the horn again, then waved from behind the steering wheel. She pulled into the parking lot and stopped on the other side of the front doors.

"All aboard!" Raz called out as the doors swung open.

Mambo lined up the girls and checked everyone off her list. Nearly every kid was coming to camp, except two players from the Cow Pokes and one player from the Taco

Bout-its who already had plans with their families. Tomoko noticed how sad both of those teams looked without everyone there. She was glad she had decided to come.

Lo lifted a latch at the bottom of the bus. A section swung upward, revealing a large, empty metal box.

"Who has to ride in there?" a Cherry Pits player asked.

"No one," Lo said, laughing. "It's for your bags! Once Mambo checks you in, come drop your bag here before you head to your seats."

Tomoko shifted nervously. It was time for them to go and spend the next week with a whole group of new people. She took a deep breath and swung her bag up over her shoulders.

"You'll be great," a warm voice said in her ear.

Tomoko turned and hugged her uncle.

"Thank you, ojichan," she said.

Her mom handed Tomoko her basketball, then gave Tomoko a big hug too.

"Have fun!" she said.

"I will," Tomoko answered. She turned with the other Daredevils for the bus.

Lo pointed at Tomoko's basketball. "That coming too?"

"Yeah," Tomoko said. She blushed a little. "If I'm allowed."

Lo smiled. "We'll see how much free time y'all have to

use it," she said. "Keep it in your lap so it won't go rolling around. I don't want to see one dribble from here until Dallas."

Tomoko nodded vigorously and tucked the ball by her side as she climbed the bus steps. Shelly and Jules were already sharing one row. Bree and Kenzie were right behind them. Tomoko sighed and took an empty seat on the aisle across from Jules.

"It will be fine," Tomoko whispered to herself. She squeezed the ball to her chest. "Everything will be fine."

CHAPTER SIX

IT TOOK THE GREEN BUS FOREVER TO CREEP THROUGH downtown Austin. Tomoko stared out the window, imagining all the cars honking were a collection of voices saying *Stay home! Stay home!*

She shook the thought from her head.

Finally, Raz steered the bus onto the highway. The league sailed out of Austin, heading into some bit of unknown wilderness near Dallas.

Tomoko tapped on her basketball.

"Want to play more derby basketball at camp?" Jules asked.

Tomoko looked across the aisle. "If we have time," she said. "But Lo said we might not get around to it. I guess between hiking and derby drills, we'll be really busy."

Shelly leaned her head over Jules's lap. "How much hiking do you think they'll make us do?"

Tomoko shrugged. "My uncle Randall and I usually hike between two and five miles a day when we go camping."

Shelly's eyes bugged out. "Five *miles?*"

"Yeah," Tomoko said. "But we're always out looking for birds or snakes or whatever. It's not like we carry our packs that far."

"I could barely lug mine from the car to the bus," Jules said. "Window fans are really heavy."

"Window fans?" Tomoko shook her head. She couldn't tell if Jules was being serious. "As in, the big things you plug into the wall?"

"Well, yeah," Jules said. "Duh. If it's going to be as hot in Dallas as it is in Austin, then I want a fan!"

Tomoko shifted in her seat so she was facing Jules and Shelly head-on. She let the ball roll between her back and the bus bench.

"Jules," Tomoko said carefully, "there are no electrical outlets when you're camping."

Jules cocked her head. "What about for fans?" she asked. "Or our cell phones?"

"We'll probably have to turn our phones off once we get there and call our parents," Tomoko explained, "so we don't waste the battery. As for staying cool, there's lots of easy ways that don't involve fans!"

Two players from the Shady Birds twisted their heads around to look at Tomoko from their own bench.

"Like what?" they asked.

Tomoko shrugged. "You can bring some bandanas to a water source and soak them, then tie them around your neck."

"I didn't bring any bandanas," Kenzie said.

Bree stuck out her tongue. "I don't want to dunk my stuff in a pond anyway. There's probably fish pee in there."

"My uncle and I get our drinking water from rivers when we're camping," Tomoko said. "We mix a little iodine in our canteens to clean the water."

Now more derby players were sitting up and turning toward Tomoko.

"You know a lot about this stuff, huh," a Cherry Pits player said.

Tomoko smiled. "I mean . . . I like to go camping."

"Thank goodness you're coming!" Shelly said. "I'd be totally lost up in the woods without you. I'd probably roller-skate right into a tree or something."

Everyone in their section of the bus laughed.

"What do you do when you and your uncle find snakes?"
another girl asked.

"We catch them!" Tomoko said.

The girls all gasped. They leaned in as Tomoko told them
about slinging indigo snakes over her shoulders and following vermillion flycatcher birds between branches. As the
bus ride went on, Tomoko was starting to feel like she might
be even more confident in Dallas than she had ever been in
Austin! She hoped the derby players on the Dallas league
would be as interested in camping as everyone else on
the bus.

Mambo cupped her hands around her mouth.

"We'll be there in T-minus fifteen minutes!" she called. "Gather your pillows, blankets, and snacks so we make it off the bus before the sun sets!"

"That's to make sure we have time to pitch our tents," Tomoko murmured to the players around her.

"I didn't bring a tent!" Shelly cried.

"Don't worry," Tomoko said. "They'll bring tents for all of us. My uncle always takes care of that kind of stuff."

Tomoko turned out the window. More and more signs were lining up on the sides of the highway.

EXIT NOW FOR A PAIR OF FAMOUS COWBOY BOOTS!

STOP IN AT SILVESTER'S STEAKHOUSE!

THE DALLAS RANCH HOTEL WELCOMES YOU!

"Huh," Tomoko said. That was strange. They seemed to be going right through the middle of the city.

Maybe the camp was on the other side of Dallas, and they had to get through a bunch of traffic first.

She watched as Raz changed lanes. The green bus steered into the exit toward the steakhouse. They dipped under a bridge and were back on the same types of roads they had been on in Austin. Other cars clustered around them.

The other derby players folded their blankets and

emptied their bags of chip crumbs into their mouths. Tomoko squeezed her basketball as she watched the buildings around them grow taller and taller. A road sign out her window told her they were heading into the downtown area of Dallas.

"OK, players," Lo said. "Almost there!"

Almost there? Tomoko raised an eyebrow. But they weren't even close to a campground or river. The only trees in sight grew in sidewalk plots!

The bus twisted down a smaller side road. It went past a park with a basketball court, but this court looked nothing like the one Tomoko knew back home. It turned down a street with lots of small shops, but none of them were the pizza shop or juice bar or taco stands that Tomoko knew. The bus went by tall skyscrapers with shapes that were completely unfamiliar. The windows of the buildings rose up and up and up, crowding out the sun even more than the tallest trees in the woods.

Tomoko waited for them to turn back for the highway, or onto a small dirt road with a river running alongside it. But the bus turned down one last street filled with more tall buildings before it stopped, smack in the middle of the city. There were crowds of strangers hurrying along the sidewalk.

"Made it!" Raz said.

"Grab all your stuff and leave those seats clean!" Mambo called. She picked up her clipboard and took the three steps down off the bus.

Tomoko's hands shook a little as she pulled her basketball up behind her. She had never heard of a camp like this before. Suddenly, all of her stories about catching snakes and spotting birds seemed so silly. She shuffled off the bus behind the other Daredevils.

The sun was dropping fast as Lo opened the bottom of the bus compartment and began handing out bags. Tomoko watched as each girl grabbed her duffel and slung it over her arm. She could see her hiking backpack sticking out like a sore thumb in the pile. She wanted to hide it away from everyone.

"Tomoko!" Lo said. She yanked the top strap of the pack toward her. "Step right up!"

Tomoko frowned as she grabbed the straps. The backpack was meant for spending days in the woods. She had tied her sleeping bag to the top of the pack and her sleeping pad to the bottom.

Tomoko looked around at the other bags. No one had brought a sleeping bag or sleeping pad except for her.

Lo slammed the compartment door shut and slapped the bus twice. Raz gave a thumbs-up from the driver's seat and switched the bus on until it was jerking and shaking as hard as Tomoko's stomach.

"Raz will catch up once she parks in the main lot," Mambo said. "Let's go inside and meet the Dallas league!"

She pointed toward the double doors of a tall building.

Dallas Downtown Convention Center was engraved along the front.

Shelly turned back to Tomoko and smiled. "Guess we don't have to set up tents after all," she said cheerily.

Tomoko swallowed. "Guess not."

They filed into the building. Tomoko had to duck just to make sure her pack didn't catch on any of the doorframes. The league filtered down the hall, their footsteps echoing over the tile.

"Almost," Mambo said.

They dipped down one last hallway that led to another set of double doors.

"Aha, here we are." Mambo and Lo pulled the doors open. "Head right inside!"

Tomoko and the Daredevils walked into what looked like another roller-skating warehouse. Several more doors were on the far wall, with words like *Bathroom, Lockers,* and *Bunks* painted over the doorways.

Around thirty girls were skating on the track. They paused as the Austin league shuffled through.

"Check out Wilderness Girl over there," a Dallas player said. Several girls around her chuckled.

Tomoko hunched her shoulders in as tight as she could squeeze them. The league had barely arrived and already Tomoko was standing out, but not in the way that she had wanted.

She wished she could turn her whole self invisible along with her backpack.

CHAPTER SEVEN

TOMOKO QUICKLY LEARNED THAT DERBY CAMPING WAS *nothing* like the camping she was used to.

Instead of tamping down dirt, setting up tents between trees, and unrolling sleeping bags, the Austin league skaters were led to a large room inside the Dallas warehouse with bunk beds stacked all the way to the back wall.

"Usually the Dallas league uses this room for their own players," Mambo Rambo told the girls, "but this summer they're sharing it with us."

"Wow." Shelly threw her bag onto a high bunk. "That's lucky!"

Tomoko wasn't sure if she would call how everything turned out "lucky." She stuffed her sleeping bag and sleeping pad under the lowest bunk in the far corner. The mattress on the bunk was plastic and crinkly. The sheets were stiff and itchy. She sighed as she snuggled in the first night. She thought about her uncle going camping without her.

The next day, Tomoko and the other Daredevils woke up to a pair of crashing cymbals. Lo grinned as she peered over them.

"A Dallas coach let me borrow these," she said. "Time for meals, then wheels! Let's go! Up and at 'em!"

Jules's upside-down head popped over Tomoko's bunk. Her frizzy hair stuck out from end to end.

"Do you think they'll let us have s'mores for breakfast?" she asked sleepily. "Since we're at derby camp?"

"Probably not," Tomoko said. She hugged her knees in close, then shimmied out of the white, starchy sheets.

The Austin league sat along the snack bar tables, spooning oatmeal and orange slices into their mouths as the members of the Dallas league slowly trickled into the warehouse.

"I remember eating breakfast here last summer," one Dallas girl said. She grimaced. "Thank goodness we get to stay home this year and eat cereal like normal people."

Tomoko let her eyes flutter back to her bowl of oatmeal. The girl was tall, like Tomoko, but her arms and legs were long and slender. She had light blond hair that nearly reached her waist. It was the player from yesterday who had called Tomoko "Wilderness Girl."

"No can of beans or fresh fish this morning?" a voice asked.

Tomoko didn't look up. Jules nudged Tomoko's side.

"I think she's talking to you," Jules whispered.

The same Dallas player was leaning over Tomoko's end of the table.

"Or maybe you'd rather have kimchi or something like that."

Now Tomoko's eyebrows rose. It was one thing to have this girl make fun of Tomoko's hiking backpack. But why would she bring up kimchi?

"I'm Japanese American," Tomoko said. "Kimchi is a Korean dish."

"Plus, her favorite breakfast food is breakfast tacos," Kenzie said. She narrowed her eyes at the Dallas player.

The girl rolled her eyes and turned away from the table. "Whatever," she said.

Tomoko slowly looked up from her bowl. The girl from Dallas was already across the warehouse, grabbing a pair of skates from the counter. The other Daredevils had gone back to eating. Tomoko felt strange. What had just happened? Why had that girl gone out of her way to be mean?

"Should I, um . . ." Tomoko set down her spoon. "Should I tell someone?"

"Tell someone what?" Shelly asked. "That we want breakfast tacos?"

"No," Tomoko said. She scanned the table, trying to see if any of her teammates seemed as upset about the girl as she was.

Bree met Tomoko's gaze and shook her head slightly.

"Show her up on the track," Bree said. She ripped another slice from her orange.

Tomoko nodded, though her heart still twisted inside her chest. Derby camp had barely started and already she was being treated like an outsider.

Both the Austin and Dallas coaches had the girls running derby drills all day long. They broke and had sandwiches for lunch, then hot dogs and veggie burgers for dinner. Whenever they weren't stuffing food into their mouths or guzzling down water, they were panting along the track.

"Pushcarts! Team up! One Austin player with one Dallas player!"

Ffftt!

Mambo blew the whistle and clapped her hands.

Tomoko watched Jules wave to one girl, then turned as Kenzie skated over to another. Two by two, the leagues were pairing off and finding spots over the track. The Dallas league thinned out until only one girl was left staring at Tomoko.

"Oh no," Tomoko whispered.

She turned toward her teammates. Someone would have to see and offer to swap partners. But none of the other Daredevils looked over.

"Looks like it's you and me, Wilderness Girl," the Dallas player said.

"Tomoko," Tomoko murmured. "My name's Tomoko."

"I can't pronounce that," the girl said. "Plus, I think Wilderness Girl's better. I'm Emma. I'll push first."

Tomoko sighed as Emma pivoted around. Her hands felt stiff on Tomoko's back.

"Here we go," Emma said.

Mambo blew the whistle again. Emma's hands dug into Tomoko. She was pushing a lot harder than Tomoko had

expected. The pair veered sideways. Tomoko slammed into the railing.

Ffftttt!

Raz and a Dallas coach skated over.

"You OK, Tomonater?" Raz asked.

Tomoko rubbed her side. She caught her breath.

"Whoops," Emma said cheerfully. "I think I might've

pushed too hard. I just wasn't sure how much it would take to get her rolling."

Tomoko's cheeks went bright red. She turned to see if Shelly was breathing like an angry dragon or if Jules was getting ready to unleash a "Hi-yah!" hip check on the girl. But her teammates all seemed busy talking to their new partners from Dallas. Raz narrowed her eyes at Emma for a moment, then blew her whistle twice and pointed at the jammer line.

Tomoko's head slumped as she skated back to Emma for another round of pushcarts.

"Melody is so great," Shelly said that night as the girls changed into pajamas and brushed their teeth in the locker bathrooms. "She tells the best jokes. Have you heard the one about the anteater and the pickles?"

"I heard her tell it to you," Bree said. She laughed. "My partner was awesome too. She said she's going to bring in these really cool fringe earrings she and her mom make together. Maybe I can get a booth set up for her jewelry at our next bout in Austin!"

Kenzie told the Daredevils how her partner had a little brother, and they spent most of the afternoon discussing which was harder, little sisters or little brothers. Kenzie insisted that dealing with Verona was way harder than having your hair ties occasionally flushed down the toilet.

Jules talked about a new "windmill" move she made up with her Dallas partner and how if they ever end up on the same team, they're going to knock out every blocker on the track.

"What about you, Tomoko?" Shelly asked. "How were drills?"

Tomoko shrugged. "Fine," she mumbled.

She was too embarrassed to talk about how Emma had said Tomoko was hard to push around.

Tomoko wondered why she didn't find a new friend the way all her teammates did. Was there a reason her partner had been so mean?

She also wondered why no one else seemed to notice how hard Tomoko's day had been. She remembered the panicky feeling she got at the Barton Springs pool, when the other Daredevils had left her behind so they could make it over to the water. It felt like they were all leaving her behind now.

"Good night!" Kenzie called from her bunk.

"Night!" Bree said.

"Sweet snoozes," Jules added.

Shelly laughed. "But don't actually snore."

Tomoko laid there with her head on the pillow. She didn't say anything.

She rolled over and thought of the summer she had planned in Austin filled with derby basketball. She thought of the summer her uncle had planned with their annual camping trip to South Texas. She pictured herself in Austin, then with her uncle, proud and stepping up to lead.

Tomoko sighed. She wished she could be that person here in Dallas too.

CHAPTER EIGHT

TOMOKO TRIED HARD TO HARNESS HER LEADER energy, but the rest of the week at derby camp seemed to go just like the first day.

Kenzie, Shelly, Bree, and Jules kept learning more and more about some of the Dallas league skaters with every drill and scrimmage. They were making new friends and sharing stories every night in the bunk room.

Meanwhile, Tomoko didn't have any stories to share. Or rather, she didn't have any stories she wanted to share.

While Jules was getting new bruises from hip checks, Tomoko's heart was getting bruised by the snide comments Emma passed to her while lacing up on the benches. The other girls were making new memories on the track, but

Tomoko was just trying to hold on to all her great memories with the team before coming out to Dallas.

"Blocking drill!" Mambo called on the second to last day. "Team blockers can stay together for this one. I want all the main jammers from each team to line up over here!"

Bree made a salute and took off to the jammer line. Each team of blockers waited their turn to take on the track. When one team's blockers were up, the whole line of jammers tried to skate through the pack, one after the other. The blockers were supposed to keep everyone from getting through, even their own team's jammer. But it was hard when one girl after the next came flying up behind them.

"Daredevils, you're up!"

The Daredevils blockers shuffled onto the rink. Tomoko looked over her shoulder. She could see Bree waiting in the jammer line. She could also see Emma in the jammer line behind Bree. Tomoko sighed and readied herself next to Kenzie.

Fffttt!

The blockers all skated forward.

"One at a time, jammers!" Mambo said. "Wait until each one gets through before heading in next!"

Fffttt!

The line of roller-skate wheels rumbled behind Tomoko. She braced herself alongside Kenzie, getting ready to throw some good blocks and hip checks on the track. It always cheered Tomoko up to work with her team. And Bree was right—if Tomoko was going to show up Emma anywhere, it should be on the track.

The first jammer caught up with the pack. Jules and Shelly jutted their shoulders to the side, trying to keep the jammer behind them. The girl made it to Kenzie and Tomoko. Tomoko leaned into the pack, forcing the jammer closer to Kenzie, who shifted her hips and landed a firm hip check.

"Jammer down!" Raz said. "Next!"

Another jammer came flying down the track. This time, all four Daredevils blockers zipped and shifted and moved, keeping the jammer behind them.

"Nice blocking!" Lo called. "Go ahead and let the jammer through. Next!"

One by one, the jammer line sailed into the Daredevils pack. Tomoko, Kenzie, Jules, and Shelly all worked together to keep the jammers behind them or send them down with hip checks. Tomoko smiled. She was starting to feel like her old self.

"Next jammer!" Lo said.

Tomoko heard the familiar *clack clack clack*-ing of Bree's skates. The Daredevils worked on lots of practices where they blocked Bree instead of letting her through. Tomoko knew how Bree liked to skate through the pack. She prepared for Bree to reach them.

But as Bree got to the pack, there was another rumbling sound over the rink.

Tomoko nudged into Bree's side to keep her from passing. Bree nudged back into Tomoko.

Suddenly Tomoko felt a hard jab on her other side. She was still off balance from leaning into Bree. Tomoko wobbled back and forth. She tried to steady herself. Another jab came into her side.

"Ow!" Tomoko cried. She dropped down onto her knees.

Ffftttt!

All the skaters on the track came to a halt. Tomoko blinked and looked up. She could see Kenzie, Jules, and Shelly in front of her. She could also see Bree . . . and Emma.

"I said one jammer at a time," Mambo said. She turned to Emma.

"Sorry," Emma said. She shrugged. "I couldn't see the other girl anymore. I thought you called me up."

"She's right here!" Kenzie held both hands out toward Bree. "How could you not see her?"

Shelly leaned over Tomoko. Her face was creased with worry.

"What happened?" Shelly whispered.

"I think she elbowed me," Tomoko said. She closed her eyes. She did not want to cry on the track.

Shelly popped up. "Penalty!" she shouted. She pointed at Emma. "Elbow contact! Twice! That's gotta be a major penalty, right? Where's the penalty box?"

Lo held out her hands. "Calm down, Bomb Shell. There is no penalty box. We're just practicing right now. We're learning from mistakes so we don't make them in bouts."

"She hurt the Tomonater!" Shelly said.

Mambo cocked her head and looked at Tomoko. "Is that true?"

Tomoko stood next to Shelly. She bit her lip. If she told on Emma, she would look like the biggest baby on the track, not a leader. Plus, what if the other coaches didn't believe her?

Tomoko shrugged. "I don't know."

Mambo and Lo looked at each other.

"That's probably enough for today," Mambo said. She blew her whistle again. "Dinner in thirty! Then we'll go over the schedule for the end-of-camp derby extravaganza tomorrow!"

The rest of both leagues whooped and cheered as the

Daredevils and other jammers skated off the track. Tomoko didn't say much of anything as she unclipped her helmet and took off her knee and elbow pads. She was silent as she slipped her feet out of her skates and changed into sneakers.

Shelly and Bree watched Tomoko push her food around with her fork during dinner. They traded looks with each other.

"I was just talking to Mambo," Bree said to the other Daredevils. "And she told me that until the extravaganza tomorrow afternoon, we get the day for free practice. We basically get to do whatever we want!"

"Cool," Kenzie said. "What should we do?"

Tomoko shoved some corn across her plate.

"Well, I was trying to figure out a way to get some time on our own," Bree said.

Tomoko glanced across the table. "And?"

"And I got an idea," Bree said. She lowered her voice. "I say we go have our practice somewhere *outside* the rink."

Kenzie and Shelly's eyebrows went up. Jules rubbed her hands together.

"Like where?" Jules asked.

"Remember that park on the way in?" Bree asked. "There was a basketball court on it. Tomoko, I was thinking we could use your ball and play some derby basketball together as a team. What do you think?"

Tomoko smiled at Bree. Her side was still sore from Emma's jabs that afternoon. Her heart was still sore from Emma's jabs all week. But getting to spend some time with just the Daredevils was exactly what she needed.

"OK," Tomoko said. "Let's do it."

Bree grinned and placed her palm flat on the table. Tomoko placed her hand over Bree's. Jules stacked hers on next, then Shelly, then Kenzie.

"Operation park hooky!" Jules whispered.

"Operation derby basketball," Bree said.

The Daredevils raised their hands and picked up their forks. This time Tomoko swallowed a big bite of corn.

CHAPTER NINE

THE NEXT MORNING, TOMOKO WAS WORRIED THAT SHE had dreamed up Bree's idea about playing basketball at the park. But as Tomoko sat at their regular table for breakfast, she found the other Daredevils discussing their plan of escape.

"How about I cause a big commotion to distract people?" Jules said. "Then you guys can all run off and I'll slip out and meet you outside."

Kenzie shook her head. "How are you supposed to slip out if you cause a big commotion?"

Jules shrugged. "In cartoons, whenever there's a big commotion, everyone comes together and makes a cloud of dust."

She wiggled her fingers and curled her hands like she was holding an invisible ball.

"That's what this would be like. Then while everyone's freaking out, I just crawl between their feet and run off!"

Bree rolled her eyes. "How about there are no commotions. Commotions are not part of our plan."

"Fine." Jules hunched over her breakfast tray.

"Hey Tomonater," Shelly said. She perked up as Tomoko sat down. "We're just figuring out how to get away after breakfast."

Tomoko nodded and took a bite of her toast.

"Any ideas?" Kenzie asked.

Tomoko scrunched up her mouth. "No. Sorry."

"That's OK," Bree said. "I've actually been working on something. What do you think about this—"

She leaned in close to the other Daredevils members. Tomoko planted her elbows on the table and listened.

"Once we finish eating breakfast, we'll tell Mambo that we want to practice a secret move for the extravaganza this afternoon. I'll mention that I saw another room down the hall when we came in and ask if we can go there. Then we'll head to the park."

"What if someone goes looking for us?" Kenzie asked.

Bree held her arms out. "It's a huge building! They'll just think we went to a room farther away! Plus, we'll be back before anyone goes looking for us."

"What about our real move for the extravaganza?" Shelly added.

Kenzie swiped the air. "We have lots of secret Daredevils moves to use for that."

"Maybe we can even use a basketball move," Bree said. She grinned at Tomoko. Tomoko smiled and blushed.

Jules drummed her fingers on the snack bar table.

"I think my idea is more fun," she said. "But I like yours too, Bree."

"Great," Bree said. She clapped her hands together. "It's settled. Grab skates and elbow pads, everyone. I'll go get my phone, then sweet-talk Mambo."

Twenty minutes later, the Daredevils were rumbling down the long, tiled halls decked out in skating gear. Tomoko had her basketball carefully tucked by her side. The convention center was even more gargantuan than she had remembered from when the league arrived a week ago.

"There are tons of rooms here," Bree said. "It's even bigger than I thought!"

Shelly tugged at a strap on her elbow pad. "Mambo said to take the first right and to go down to the end of the hall."

Bree flicked her hand. "It's super easy to get lost with those kind of directions. That buys us at least a couple hours for sure! Come on."

She steered the group to the left, down a particularly wide hallway with long windows at the far end. She held her cell phone in front of her like she was holding a trail map.

"OK," Bree said. "All we do is take a right on the sidewalk, go down four blocks, another left, fast right, and boom—we're there."

The Daredevils emerged from the main front doors. The downtown buildings towered over them, casting the entire street in shadow. Kenzie tilted her head far back as she gazed at the high rising towers.

"I'm glad you brought your phone," Kenzie said.

Bree waved her arms like a traffic controller, directing the Daredevils over crosswalks and down side streets. Tomoko kept her basketball close. The buildings were so tall and dark. They reminded her of the giant redwood trees in California, where her uncle Randall had brought her when she was younger. She felt so small wandering between them.

"Just a little bit farther . . . and . . . here!" Bree said. She looked up from her phone.

Tomoko looked up with Bree. Only one block from where they stood, they could see a park waiting like an island in between the buildings.

The Daredevils turned to one another.

"All right!" Shelly said. She offered Bree a high five. "You did it!"

"Thank you, thank you." Bree bowed over and over. She twisted her hand above her head with a flourish. She moved one skate behind the other to curtsy, then lost her footing. Kenzie grabbed Bree's elbow.

"We get it," Kenzie said, laughing. "You're awesome. Now let's practice some derby basketball!"

The team went to a crosswalk and waited their turn at the light. Tomoko could hardly wait to be on the court again. Sure, the park wasn't really like their park in Austin. And the basketball court didn't have the helpful lines painted over each section like the one at home. But she had her friends with her, and they were playing her two favorite things: roller derby and basketball.

Tomoko could still be a leader on the court.

Once the Daredevils were safely across, they spread themselves over the basketball court. Tomoko directed Kenzie and Shelly on either side of the hoop. She and Jules took the mid-court lines. Tomoko bounced the basketball to Bree.

"You start," Tomoko said. "Since you got us here."

Bree caught the ball, then tucked her phone under a side bench.

"Ready," she said.

Bree dribbled the basketball to the midline. Jules made a quick lunge for Bree and landed on her knees. Tomoko skated over and smacked the basketball out of Bree's hands. She dribbled down the other side of the court and sunk the ball—nothing but net.

"That was awesome!" Bree said.

Tomoko beamed. "Maybe Kenzie can have the ball next, and this time I'll stand under the hoop," she said.

The Daredevils passed the basketball to each member as they set up for drills again and again. They played where they all blocked the one with the basketball, just like how they all blocked one jammer during derby bouts. They played two on three, the way teams usually played each other in basketball. They even played a game Shelly made up where the person holding the basketball could "explode" over the court, which meant they got to throw the ball at an opposing player to knock them down. Tomoko suspected Shelly especially loved playing that way since she was known as the exploding Bomb Shell on the track.

"Hey," Bree said as the girls wound down Shelly's game. "I actually have an idea for how we could use this for the extravaganza."

"What is it?" Jules asked. She twirled Tomoko's basketball. "I don't think they'll let us throw things at each other."

"No," Bree said. "I was thinking about switching jammers! You know how Lo told us that in jams the jammer can pass their star helmet panty to another team member?"

"Only the pivot," Kenzie said. "That's the blocker who wears a helmet panty with a stripe on it."

"Fine, the pivot then," Bree said. She swiped the basketball from Jules. "Well, let's just pretend this ball is the jammer panty. I can get it to the pack super fast. But then we could practice passing it on and another player taking over as jammer."

"The Tomonater would be perfect for that!" Shelly said.

Tomoko's eyebrows went up. "I would?"

"Of course," Shelly said. "You're awesome when it comes to passes, or really anything that combines derby skills with basketball skills!"

The other Daredevils grinned and nodded.

"Sweet," Bree said. "It's settled. Tomoko can be the pivot during the extravaganza. Let's go back and really show off to the others!"

She tossed the basketball to Tomoko and turned for the bench.

Tomoko beamed as she caught the ball. She couldn't wait to wear the special pivot panty over her helmet. In derby, being a pivot was like being leader of the blockers. She would get to step up at camp after all.

"Wow," Kenzie said. She squinted at the looming buildings. "It's so hard to find your way around here. I don't even remember which side we came from!"

"Hmmm . . ." Jules narrowed her eyes and spun in a circle. "It was definitely one of these ways." She pointed her fingers in two opposite directions.

Shelly laughed. "That's why they invented cell phones with GPS," she said. She turned to Bree. "You coming?"

Bree didn't answer. Tomoko and the others all turned along with Shelly. Bree was on her hands and knees, pulling tufts of grass from the ground.

"No, no, no," Bree muttered.

"Um . . . everything OK over there?" Jules asked.

Kenzie skated to Bree. "What's going on?"

Bree turned to the group. Her eyes were wide.

"My phone," she said. She let a fistful of grass float away on the breeze. "It's gone."

CHAPTER TEN

"WAIT," KENZIE SAID. SHE FURROWED HER EYEBROWS. "What do you mean it's gone?"

"I left it right here!" Bree said. She waved her arms up and down frantically over the area below the bench. "Do you see it now? No! It's gone! Poof! Into thin air!"

"But we've been here the whole time," Shelly said.

Jules sniffed. "I definitely would have sent a mean hip check to whoever tried to take it."

Bree pressed both hands into her cheeks. Her shoulders were shaking.

"It doesn't matter who took it," she said. She heaved a breath out. "What matters is we don't have it."

Kenzie tilted her head back. "And we don't know which way to go."

Jules put her hands on her hips. "Which means . . ."

" . . . we're lost," Shelly said.

Tomoko looked at each of her teammates. They all seemed scared. Usually someone was taking charge. But now they were just as quiet as Tomoko. She turned and looked at the buildings around them.

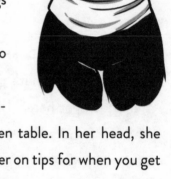

They remind me of trees, Tomoko thought to herself.

She pictured her uncle Randall's field guide from the kitchen table. In her head, she peeled the pages open to a chapter on tips for when you get lost in a patch of really tall trees.

- **Look for which side the moss grows on tree trunks.**

- **Check for signs of animal trails.**

- **Stay close to moving water if possible.**

- **If you see other hikers, trade information.**

Tomoko sighed. Her tips for finding her way in the woods weren't going to help now. She was just as stuck as everyone else.

"Hey!" Shelly brightened and pointed her finger in the air. "I know what we can do."

"What?" Kenzie asked. She kept one hand on Bree's shoulder. Bree was still crouched next to the bench.

"It's easy," Shelly said. "Sometimes when I walk with my mom to art class, she's too tired to walk home and we end up calling a ride! Let's do that and just tell them to drop us off at the convention center."

"We need a phone to call them!" Bree cried. She yanked another handful of grass.

"Come on," Kenzie murmured to Bree. "Stand next to me. It's OK."

Bree huffed and groaned as she pushed herself up on her skates. Her eyes were red.

"We don't have to call anyone," Shelly said. "You can also just put your hand up and a cab stops, no problem. I've seen it in movies. Come on!"

Shelly waved and turned to one end of the park.

Tomoko squinted. Something seemed unfamiliar about the direction Shelly was heading. Did she know which way they had taken to get here? Tomoko checked the other sides of the basketball court and playground. It was so hard to tell if she was remembering correctly. Plus, she didn't want to be the one who got everyone even *more* lost. Tomoko shook her head and followed Shelly and the others toward the curb.

Shelly held her arm up in the air. She watched hopefully as one car after another came zooming down the road.

"You sure this is a good idea, Bomb Shell?" Kenzie asked.

"Uh-huh," Shelly said. "A cab will take us back, easy! We can kick our skates up and relax!"

The Daredevils craned their heads as they watched the cars pass by. None of the drivers seemed to care that Shelly's arm was still waving over her head. Tomoko was starting to worry they would all be standing there for hours.

Finally, a yellow car that said *Texas Cab* stopped in front of the girls. Shelly clapped her hands and grinned. Tomoko frowned at the back seat. It didn't look like there were enough seat belts for all five of them.

"Where you heading?" the driver asked. He leaned out of his window.

"The convention center!" Shelly said. She went to open the back door.

"Hold on one second." The driver twisted his neck as he looked at all five Daredevils. "You got money?"

"Oh," Shelly said. She turned to her teammates. "Do you have money?" she whispered.

Bree, Kenzie, and Tomoko shook their heads.

"I've got like five dollars," Jules said.

"Nuts." Shelly put a hand to her chin and thought a moment, then snapped her fingers. She turned again to the driver. "We have money! It's just back at the convention center! We'll pay you after you drop us off."

The cab driver did not look as excited about Shelly's plan.

"No money, no ride," he said.

Before Shelly could say anything, the cab revved up and took off down the road.

Shelly watched as the car disappeared down the block. She balled her hands up into tight fists.

"Well, sheesh!" she cried out. "Doesn't anybody trust people anymore?"

"Don't worry about it," Jules said. "You actually gave me a great plan! Maybe five dollars isn't enough for a cab ride, but it's got to be enough for the bus. We'll just go to the nearest stop and get off once it passes by the convention center!"

Tomoko pressed her lips together. The reason why the field guide said to stay near moving water when you were lost was so that you only went in one direction. But didn't buses go in all sorts of directions? What if they ended up hopping on a bus that took them to the other side of the city?

But Jules and the others were already rolling along the sidewalk to the nearest crosswalk. Tomoko sighed and rolled after them.

"Over there!" Jules said. She pointed another block away. "I see a bus stop!"

Tomoko looked over her shoulder. The park was nearly out of view. She remembered reading something about staying in one spot, if you were truly lost in the woods. Then again, Jules had a plan to get them out of this mess. And the city was *not* the same as the woods. So maybe staying at the park wasn't all that important.

The Daredevils gathered around a bench with a huge laminated map that said *DART* along the bottom.

Dallas Area Rapid Transit

"OK," Jules said. She squinted at the map. A bunch of different colored lines intersected over and over.

"Where are the street names? Or the buildings?" Shelly asked. "There's not even a *You are here* sign!"

"Relax," Jules said. "Just because your plan didn't work, doesn't mean you have to stomp all over mine."

Jules leaned closer to the map. Tomoko watched Jules carefully. Jules cocked her head back and forth. She placed a finger along one of the colored lines and followed its wiggly pattern through the city, frowning.

"Maybe if we . . ." Jules's voice faded as she spoke.

"Maybe if we what?" Kenzie asked.

"Hold on a second!" Jules said. "I'm thinking!"

Shelly slapped a hand on her forehead. "You are not. You're just as confused as the rest of us!"

Jules huffed and turned to Shelly. "Well, what do you want to do? Use your pretend money for another cab? That worked out great."

"It is not pretend money!" Shelly said. "I have real money, it's back at the convention center."

Shelly and Jules glared at each other. Kenzie shook her head and closed her eyes. Bree barely looked up from the sidewalk. She had seemed totally out of it since her phone went missing.

Tomoko's heart flopped as she looked at her friends. There was a phrase her uncle Randall liked to use whenever something went wrong during their camping trips. He said it was like being in a boat without a paddle. The Daredevils always had at least one person who would steer and paddle the rest of the team along. But now everything was falling apart. They were drifting everywhere and nowhere at the same time.

Tomoko hunched her shoulders. She wished she knew what to do, but she was just as paddle-less as everyone else.

CHAPTER ELEVEN

JULES SQUINTED AT THE SLICES OF SKY PEEKING OUT between the buildings.

"Anyone know what time it is?" she asked.

Shelly folded her arms. "Not without a phone," she said.

Bree didn't say anything.

Tomoko tilted her head back and gazed up at the sky along with Jules. Whenever she and her uncle Randall went camping, they didn't take phones—or even watches—with them. Randall had taught Tomoko how to tell basic time based on what position the sun was in the sky.

It was hard to see the sun from where the girls were standing. But the sun was a really powerful thing. You didn't have to see it exactly to know where it was coming from.

There! Tomoko thought. She saw a spray of thick sun rays

spring out from a cloud. The sun looked like it was positioned near the center of the sky, which would make the time around noon.

Tomoko turned to the others.

"I may know—"

"Hey!" Kenzie said. She snapped her fingers. "I have an idea."

Tomoko closed her mouth. Kenzilla was the main planner of the Daredevils—Crown Jules had even officially dubbed her as the mastermind of the team after their first tournament two months ago. Kenzie's idea would probably be a lot better than some facts about the sun.

"What's the idea?" Shelly asked.

"Jules," Kenzie said, "you said you had five dollars, right?"

"Yeah," Jules said. She dug her toe stop into the pavement. "A lot of good that does us now."

Tomoko looked to Kenzie eagerly. Kenzie was so good at coming up with genius plans no one else would think of. She probably knew the perfect way to get them all back with five dollars.

Kenzie nodded at Jules. "I was thinking we could use the money to buy some snacks while we're out here."

Tomoko blinked. *That* was Kenzie's great plan?

"What should we get?" Jules asked.

Kenzie shrugged. "I don't know. A bag of chips and a candy bar or something."

Tomoko thought of what Randall had taught her about what to eat during long afternoons spent in the woods.

Choose your snacks well, Randall would say. They always packed plenty of water and gorp for their hikes. *G.O.R.P.* stood for "good old raisins and peanuts." It gave hikers lots of energy while out on the trails.

"Maybe we should get some nuts," Tomoko murmured. "For protein."

"Good thinking," Kenzie said. "We'll make sure to get a candy bar with nuts in it!"

Tomoko sighed. She followed Kenzie down the block past the bus stop, then down another block and another as they searched for a convenience store. The park fell farther behind them.

"Jeez," Kenzie said. "You think they'd have a lot more shops, with so many people working here! My dad works downtown in Austin, and he loves getting snacks during his lunch breaks. He even told me he forgets my mom's packed lunches on purpose sometimes so he can grab a hot pretzel instead."

Jules shielded her eyes as she looked at the windows lining the tall buildings.

"Maybe the people who work here like packed lunches better."

"Maybe," Kenzie said.

She led the Daredevils down another block. Tomoko did

a little check over her shoulder each time they changed directions. When she was out in the woods, she was always looking for signs she might remember if they came back to that spot, like a broken branch or a weird rock formation.

Mailbox that looks like a robot, Tomoko thought at one corner.

Green paint spilled over sidewalk.

Window with giant teddy bear display.

The signs she was collecting now were not at all like the ones she looked for when she was out camping. Still, Tomoko figured it couldn't hurt to keep little bits of information like that in her back pocket.

"I see a store!" Kenzie yelled from the front of the line. "This way."

The Daredevils snaked around another block.

"I hope they have the good, spicy kind of chips," Jules said. "I hate it when they only have plain."

Tomoko shook her head. Spicy chips meant they would get thirsty fast, and it didn't seem like Kenzie was budgeting for any kind of drink. Still, she shrugged and skated through the front door.

A set of bells jingled as they all filed inside.

"Ah," Shelly said. "It's so nice and cool. Let's hang out here forever."

"That won't get us back in time for the extravaganza," Kenzie said. "But snacks will help. Come on."

They rolled into an aisle. The cashier eyed the girls' skates skeptically.

"Hey!" Kenzie whispered. She ducked down and leaned toward the others. "There's a phone on the counter!"

"Is it my phone?" Bree suddenly piped up. It was the first time she had spoken since her freak-out at the park.

"No," Kenzie said. She put a hand on Bree's elbow. "It's one of those old-school phones, not a cell phone. But we can use it to get back!"

"How?" Shelly asked. "Even if we call a cab, no one will drive us back for free."

"Maybe we can call the convention center," Jules said. "And Raz can come pick us up in the bus."

Kenzie shook her head. "No way. We'll be in tons of trouble! We can still make it back before they know we're missing."

Tomoko scrunched up her nose. She wasn't sure if Kenzie's new plan was any better than her snack plan. Still, she waited to see who Kenzie had in mind for calling.

"So who are you going to call?" Jules asked.

"I have a cousin who lives near Dallas," Kenzie said. "Maybe they'll come pick us up!"

Kenzie rolled over to the cashier. The man gazed down at Kenzie's hands—which were holding nothing—and frowned.

"Can I help you?" he asked.

"We'd like you use your phone, please," Kenzie said. She shot the man a big grin. "Real quick."

He sighed and nudged the phone toward them. Kenzie picked up the receiver and stared at the buttons. Tomoko looked at Kenzie.

"You're supposed to push them," Jules said.

Kenzie jerked her chin. "I know. I just don't remember what my cousin's phone number is."

"So call your mom or dad first," Shelly said. "And tell them you want to invite your cousin to the skating extravaganza or whatever and need their number."

"Good idea," Kenzie said. She turned and studied the buttons again.

"What is it?" Bree asked.

Kenzie rolled her head back. "I don't know my mom's phone number either, or my dad's. They're all saved on my cell phone!"

The cashier raised an eyebrow. "Something wrong?"

"Uh, no sir," Kenzie said. She pushed the phone back over to the man. "We forgot the number. Thanks anyway."

Shelly leaned over Kenzie's shoulder. She pointed to the clock on the far wall. "It's almost one p.m.!" she hissed. "They're going to start looking for us soon."

"Who is?" the cashier asked. He cocked his head. "Are you girls in some sort of trouble?"

Tomoko gulped. Kenzie pressed herself away from the counter.

"Nope, not us!" Jules said. "Trouble doesn't know us."

But the cashier didn't look convinced. "Are you lost?" he asked. "Do you need me to call someone to pick you up?"

Shelly made a sharp intake of breath.

"Busted . . ." she whispered.

Tomoko could picture Raz heaving them back onto the bus in the middle of downtown. She could see Mambo and Lo lecturing the team in front of the other players. She imagined all five Daredevils squeezing into the penalty box while everyone else got to skate in the derby extravaganza. Tomoko buried her face in her hands. Emma would have a whole new arsenal of mean things to say if they were caught now.

"Run!" Kenzie shouted.

And even though that plan wasn't great, it was the best idea Kenzie had come up with yet.

The Daredevils scrambled out of the convenience shop and rumbled down the sidewalk. Tomoko's heart pounded in her chest. She could almost hear Raz honking the horn of the green bus, chasing behind them.

CHAPTER TWELVE

AS THEY LEFT THE STORE, TOMOKO NOTICED THAT Kenzie turned the opposite way from where they had come in.

If they had still been wandering through the city, Tomoko might have suggested they try to retrace their steps. But since the Daredevils were in the middle of escaping, she said nothing.

She followed her teammates as they flew over the bumpy sidewalk. The sound of wheels roaring over the gritty pavement filled up Tomoko's ears. She watched as everyone leaned low, moving from a clump of skaters into a line as they wove between light posts and parking meters. It was some of the best skating the team had done together all summer, though that hardly seemed important now.

At some point, Bree overtook Kenzie as leader of the pack. Then Shelly was right on Bree's tail and taking over the group. Even Jules rushed to the front as the group turned a corner, gently hip checking Shelly to the side. The only one who hung back was Tomoko. She was afraid to be at the front of the group. All they had managed to do so far was tangle themselves farther into the city. Why would Tomoko jump in front just to get them even more lost?

Finally, Jules brought her skates together like a pizza slice. She slowed to a stop. Tomoko and the others toe-stopped around Jules.

"You think we're far enough away?" Shelly asked.

Kenzie nodded. She put her hands on her knees and took quick, hurried breaths. "I. Think. So."

"Whew!" Jules wiped her brow. "That was close."

Shelly made a noise that sounded like both a cough and a laugh. "We would have gotten in major trouble."

"We're still going to get in trouble."

The Daredevils turned to Bree, who had her arms folded tightly over her chest.

"It doesn't matter what happens," Bree said. "We're busted no matter what. I'm busted no matter what. Because I still don't have my phone!"

Suddenly Bree dropped her arms. She hunched over, her shoulders drooping toward the ground. She was crying, Tomoko realized.

Shelly's and Jules's eyebrows flew up. Kenzie leaned over Bree.

"Hey, it's OK," Kenzie said. "It'll be OK."

"How?" Bree wailed. She stood up straight again. Her eyes and cheeks were puffy. "How is it going to be OK? How are we supposed to get back?"

No one had an answer to that.

The girls looked around at one another. Tomoko looked at Shelly, thinking of her plan to take a cab back to derby camp. She looked at Jules, thinking of her plan to take the bus. She looked at Kenzie, thinking of her idea for getting snacks and using the phone. She looked at Bree, who had the plan to come to the park in the first place.

Everyone had come up with a plan but Tomoko. And now they needed someone to take over. They needed someone to lead them out of this mess. Tomoko remembered what Randall had said when they watched the bats fly from the bridge.

You can be like a troop leader out there!

Tomoko had been so embarrassed when they first got to Dallas. It wasn't at all like the derby camp she had imagined, and her loads of camping gear and hiking information just felt like more things people could use to make fun of her.

But now Tomoko paused and thought about that evening out with her uncle. Could all her nature know-how still come in handy, even if they were in the middle of the city?

She tilted her head back and squinted at the sky. The sun was no longer hanging around in the middle, which meant the derby extravaganza would be happening soon.

"Wait a minute," Tomoko said.

"What is it?" Kenzie asked. All the Daredevils turned to Tomoko.

Tomoko shifted her basketball to the other arm and raised her hand up. She traced a path through the clouds with her finger.

"It's heading west!" Tomoko said excitedly. "We know what direction the sun's going. So we know north, east, south, and west!"

Jules frowned. "Huh?"

Tomoko dropped her hand. "See how the sun mostly hangs out on that side of the sky? That's south. So we've been heading north this whole time. We know roughly which way the convention center is."

Shelly shielded her eyes as she gazed up at the buildings. "Whoa," she said. "That's pretty cool."

Jules looked across the circle at Tomoko. "So what does that mean, Tomonater?" she asked. "What do we do?"

Kenzie and Shelly looked at Tomoko too. Even Bree's tears dried along her cheeks as she waited to hear what Tomoko was going to say.

Tomoko took a deep breath. Maybe they didn't end up sleeping in tents like she thought. Maybe they weren't hiking on a dirt trail between a bunch of trees. But the Daredevils were still lost at camp, and they were depending on Tomoko to find their way back.

"OK," Tomoko said. She tossed her basketball to Shelly. "We're going to start with basic directions. If we want to move south, we have to go back that way."

She pointed down a sidewalk.

"We also turned down a few blocks while we were skating," Tomoko said. "Since the sun is moving west . . . I think the convention center's a little east of where we are now. It's not much, but it's a start."

Bree wiped her eyes.

"You be in front," Bree said to Tomoko.

"Yeah," Shelly said. "I'll hold on to the ball."

Tomoko nodded. She skated over to a crosswalk and waited for the light to turn. She could feel the whole team bunched up tight, waiting behind her.

She imagined one of her field guides, the pages spread open to a new trail.

Downtown Dallas, the title of the map would say.

Tomoko pictured the five Daredevils drawn out like little stick figures deep in the forest of buildings.

You are here.

There was a clear path leading to the convention center. There had to be. The Daredevils had taken a trail to get themselves stuck in the city, and there would be a trail to get them back out.

Tomoko took a deep breath. She could still be a troop leader like Randall had said. She just had to read the map in her head and use the tools her uncle had taught her.

The crosswalk sign changed to *WALK*.

Tomoko led her team across the way.

CHAPTER THIRTEEN

THE DAREDEVILS FOLLOWED BEHIND TOMOKO AS SHE waded through the tall buildings.

Tomoko tried to remember what the field guides said when you were lost in thick woods and couldn't cut right across to where you wanted to go. Instead of moving in a straight line, sometimes a hiker had to make a wiggly line by going forward, then to the side, then forward, then to the side again. Tomoko used that advice as the team crossed a road, then rolled down a block, then crossed another road.

"It's so dark downtown," Kenzie murmured as the girls waited at another crosswalk.

"Yeah," Shelly said. She spun Tomoko's basketball in her hand. "I can't even see where the sun is anymore."

"Me neither," Jules said. She turned to Tomoko. "What if we changed directions and didn't know it? It's hard to tell where anything is from here."

Tomoko squeezed one of her wrist guards. "Well, when you're in the woods and can't see the sun . . . there are these signs . . ."

"What kind of signs?" Bree asked.

Tomoko pressed her lips together. She thought back to her field guide.

· **Look for which side the moss grows on tree trunks.**

"Like moss growing on certain sides of tree trunks," Tomoko said. "It likes to grow where it can be in shadow all the time."

Jules folded her arms. "But there isn't any moss here," she said.

"Yes, but . . ." Tomoko looked around. She spotted an ice-cream cone that had landed *splat!* on the cement earlier in the day.

"There!" Tomoko said. She skated over to the ice cream. "See how there's still a sticky puddle here, but there's only a chocolate stain on that side of the light pole?"

"Gross," Shelly said.

Tomoko sighed. "The point is, the ice cream will melt on the south side of the light pole. So we're on the right track!"

"Huh," Kenzie said.

The Daredevils skated down the next block. Tomoko saw the same robot-shaped mailbox she'd noted earlier. She saw the teddy bear display. It was working! Her dreams of being a troop leader were coming true!

But not everyone seemed as excited as Tomoko.

"Are you sure we're going the right way?" Shelly asked as they all skated in line.

"Pretty sure," Tomoko said.

Shelly sped up so she was right by Tomoko's side. "But shouldn't we see the convention center by now?"

Tomoko shook her head. "We're still going over our

tracks. We already passed by the robot mailbox, so we're doing good!"

"I don't remember a robot mailbox," Kenzie said. "Plus, what if there are lots of robot mailboxes around here?"

Tomoko frowned. Was there another way of showing the team that she was doing a good job of leading them back? She pictured her field guide again.

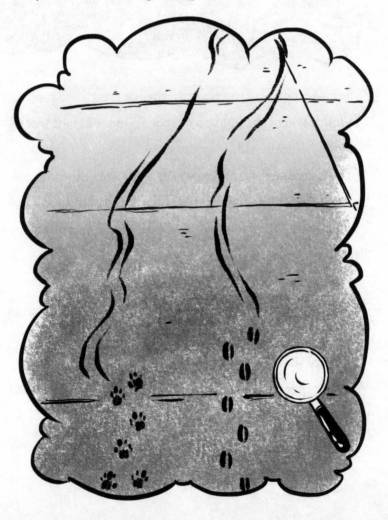

- **Check for signs of animal trails.**

"Animal trails," Tomoko murmured. "Of course!"

Bree shifted and looked at Tomoko. "Animal trails?"

"It's what you look for in the woods," Tomoko said. "When you're following an animal. But in this case the animal is us! Remember when we were skating and had to make those fast turns?"

Bree shrugged. Tomoko swept her eyes over the sidewalk.

"Like those skid marks over there!" Tomoko said, pointing. "Our wheels made those!"

She smiled as the group skated over the thin black marks scraped onto the pavement. She turned to the others, but the rest of the Daredevils still looked nervous. Even Jules started to seem a little annoyed. Tomoko's face fell. Why weren't they seeing her nature skills working?

The Daredevils continued down the block.

"I don't think we turned this much," Kenzie said as the team got ready to round another corner.

"We did, though," Tomoko said steadily. "I followed you, Jules, Shelly, and Bree the whole way out, and we did a lot of turning."

"OK," Kenzie said. She raised her arm toward a street

sign. "But what if we make a wrong turn and miss the road back to the convention center?"

Tomoko blinked at Kenzie. "Do you remember what the road was called?"

"I remember some street name," Bree said. "It was 'Main Street' or something like that."

Shelly rolled her eyes. "That's original."

Tomoko's eyes lit up. She remembered another tip from her field guide.

· stay close to moving water if possible.

The point of staying close to rivers or streams was to move along one path. If the team stuck to one street and followed it through, they wouldn't miss a turn, like Kenzie said. The street would have to take them somewhere eventually!

"OK," Tomoko said, "once we find a street we recognize, we'll take it all the way south."

"What if we don't ever recognize a street?" Shelly asked.

"We will," Tomoko said. "I will." She tried to make her voice sound extra confident. She was disappointed that her teammates didn't seem as confident in her.

But Tomoko remembered how scared she sometimes got when she and Randall were lost on the trail. Maybe it wasn't that the other Daredevils didn't believe in Tomoko. Maybe they were just too worried to realize that Tomoko's plan was working.

More and more buildings were starting to look familiar. Tomoko smiled to herself. Once she got everyone out of this mess, then they would see Tomoko as a leader too.

The group of girls continued down the sidewalk, their wheels a low grumble instead of the loud screeches and grinds from when they took off from the convenience store. Their skates no longer seemed to be shouting at others to move away or get to the side. Instead, the grumbles sounded more like a quiet protest down the alleyways and streets. The sets of wheels seemed to be asking *Are we there yet? Are we there* yet?

Suddenly Tomoko came to a halt. They had been to this corner before—she was sure of it. She gazed down the sidewalk straight ahead. She turned her head right toward a side street. Both paths looked sort of familiar.

"*Excuse* me."

Tomoko jerked her head over her shoulder. An older white woman peered over a set of cat-eye sunglasses at the Daredevils. Her eyes stopped at Tomoko. She frowned.

"You almost knocked into me, young man," the woman said.

Tomoko looked left, then right. Was the woman talking to her?

"I'm not a—"

"Wheels aren't permitted on public sidewalks," the woman said primly.

Tomoko furrowed her brow. She had been looking carefully at street signs all day long—ever since they got lost. But she didn't see anything about not being able to skate on the sidewalk.

"It's not so much of a trouble with *them*," the woman said. She waved at the other Daredevils, then sniffed. "But *certain* people need to be extra mindful of the *space* they take up."

The woman had an odd way of talking. She said one thing with her words and a second thing with her voice. Tomoko got both messages. The woman was being mean. Just like Emma at derby camp. Just like the boys playing basketball at the park, or some of the kids at school.

Tomoko turned to her teammates. They all stood there,

waiting for the crosswalk light. No one seemed to be paying attention to the woman. Tomoko had been trying to help the team. But no one was helping Tomoko.

Jules leaned into Tomoko's side.

"Ask her if the convention center's close," Jules whispered.

Tomoko's cheeks flushed red. She remembered the last tip from her guide.

- **If you see other hikers, trade information.**

In some ways, the woman was like another hiker on a trail. But in other ways, she seemed more like a dangerous predator than a source of help. Her words had felt prickly and sharp on Tomoko's skin.

"No," Tomoko muttered. "I know where we are. The center's just around that corner."

When the light turned, Tomoko skated fast away from the woman. The Daredevils sailed after her.

"What was that about?" Shelly asked.

"Nothing," Tomoko said. Her voice was low and gravelly, just like her skates.

She pumped her arms and skated faster to the corner at the far end of the block. They were almost to the convention center, she just knew it. She skated and skated until she reached the edge of the sidewalk.

Tomoko stopped.

The Daredevils nearly slammed into her.

"What is it?" Bree asked.

Tomoko couldn't answer. She motioned over her shoulder.

They had wound up at the same park they first got lost in.

CHAPTER FOURTEEN

JULES TWISTED TO PEER AROUND TOMOKO'S SIDE.

"This isn't the convention center!"

Tomoko sighed. She skated across the street, her right toe stop trailing as she rolled onto the same basketball court they had played derby ball on hours earlier.

"What gives, Tomonater?" Shelly asked. "I thought you said you knew where we were going."

"I did," Tomoko murmured. "I thought I did."

She went through all the field guide tips again in her head. The sun placement. The melted ice cream. The skate marks. The main street. She had tried so hard to make all of her camping know-how get them back in time for the extravaganza.

- **If you see other hikers, trade information.**

Tomoko's jaw tightened as she thought of the woman standing at the crosswalk. Why hadn't any of her teammates said something to the woman? They let her bully Tomoko, the same way they let Emma bully Tomoko all week.

Shelly bounced Tomoko's basketball over the court. Tomoko caught the ball and tucked it by her side. She turned away.

"Where are you going?" Kenzie asked.

Tomoko whipped around. "Away from all of you!" she said. "Everyone wanted to lead today, but nobody knows how to actually work together as a team!"

"We do too know how to be on a team," Shelly said. "It was my idea to take the cab, remember?"

"That didn't even work," Jules said. "At least I brought money for my idea."

"Oh right," Shelly said. "Which is why we're on a bus heading back to the convention center right now."

"We might have been!" Jules said. "If Kenzie hadn't made us go to the store to spend the money."

Kenzie frowned. "Well, we'd all be a lot less cranky if we had some snacks."

"Stop it!" Bree cried out. "All of you. Stop."

Kenzie, Shelly, and Jules froze. They turned to Bree.

"You didn't have any ideas at all," Jules said.

Bree folded her arms. "No, I didn't. But Tomoko did. And she's right—we barely even listened to her! Nobody trusted her."

Jules sniffed. "It's not like we're back at the convention center."

"But we are back at the park," Bree said. "Which is close to the center. Tomoko did a lot of work to get us here."

Tomoko squeezed the basketball to her side. "It's more than just that," she said.

The other Daredevils turned to her.

"What is it?" Shelly asked.

Tomoko swallowed. She had wanted to step up and be a leader for the team. She was afraid to show them how much of an outsider she had felt the whole time at camp. But as long as the Daredevils left Tomoko behind, or didn't stand up for her when people said mean things, then she would never really be a leader. Stepping up to be a leader meant asking her team to step up too.

"That woman," Tomoko said. "The one on the corner. Nobody said anything when she told me I was too big to be on the sidewalk."

Jules's eyes bugged out. "She said that?"

"She said I was taking up too much space," Tomoko murmured. Her voice was getting quiet. She hated having to talk about this. She hated it happening at all. But she wanted her teammates to be there for her.

Shelly balled up both of her fists. She spun around in a circle.

"I'm going to find that lady and show her a thing or two about derby," she said.

Tomoko held up a finger.

"It's not just the one lady, Bomb Shell. Emma, that girl at camp, has said mean things all week. But no one's said anything to her. It makes me feel like a punching bag."

Bree placed her hand on Tomoko's back.

"I know that feeling," Bree said. "When people say mean things and no one steps up. It's hard because sometimes the people who could help out aren't paying attention to what's going on. My dad calls those microaggressions."

"What's a microaggression?" Kenzie asked.

Bree turned to the group. "It's like . . . everyday mean stuff. Sometimes it doesn't sound mean even when it is.

Like if someone asks me if my hair's real. Or if I have to wear sunscreen because my skin's darker. Those may seem like regular questions, but they're actually really racist."

Kenzie's eyebrows went up.

"So that kimchi comment from the girl at camp—"

"Emma," Tomoko said. She nodded. "Yeah, that was definitely about my race. Sometimes microaggressions aren't just questions. They can be comments meant to hurt people. Like with Emma—she's made fun of my race, my weight, even my backpack. She's poked at everything."

"And we've been clueless the whole time," Shelly said. Her hands dropped their fists, deflating at her sides. "We're the worst teammates ever, Tomonater. We should have been paying more attention. We should have been listening to that lady and telling her what's what."

Tomoko gave a small smile.

"Thank you," she said.

"We also should have given you a lot more credit for getting us back here," Kenzie said. "Your camping methods really worked!"

"Do you think you could still get us to the convention center?" Jules asked.

Tomoko shrugged. "I think so."

"We can't be that far," Bree said. "I remember it only

took us like ten minutes to skate here. Of course, that was way easier when I had my phone . . ."

Bree sighed and stared into the grass. Her head snapped up.

"My phone!" she cried out. She skated off the sidewalk, her skates clomping up and down over the dirt.

"What are you doing?" Kenzie called.

Bree didn't answer. She stooped at the base of a large tree and reached into the grass.

"I found it!" Bree said. She waved her phone back and forth in the air. "Some squirrels must've moved it!"

The Daredevils cheered. Bree clomped back over, squeezing her cell phone tight.

"The battery's dead," Bree said breathlessly, but she was still smiling.

"That's OK," Jules said. "Tomoko knows what to do."

Kenzie reached for Tomoko's basketball. "Can we help you figure out where to go next?"

Tomoko looked around the park. They were standing in a tricky part of the city. Nearly every street looked the same. But Tomoko knew her skills could get them out of there. And this time, the rest of the team knew it too.

"Can anyone see the sun?" Tomoko asked.

"Not really," Shelly said.

Jules pointed. "I think it's that way."

"Great," Tomoko said. "The next thing to look for is skate tracks. Then we can narrow our options to two directions—where we just came from and where we first skated in."

"I see wheel tracks over here!" Bree said.

"And I see some this way," Kenzie said. "These ones look sort of faded."

"That's near the south side of the sky," Jules said. She looked at Tomoko. "Is that right?"

Tomoko grinned. "That's right," she said. "I think that's our way out of here."

"Let's go, then!" Shelly called. She motioned Tomoko to the front of the line.

"We've got your back," Tomoko heard Shelly say behind her. And for the first time, Tomoko finally felt like that was true.

CHAPTER FIFTEEN

TOMOKO USED THE SUN LIKE A COMPASS.

She followed the sun rays as they winked at her between the tips of the high-rise buildings. She watched for the sun's signs along the sidewalk, looking for shadows that stretched long and thin next to light poles and mailboxes.

This time, Tomoko didn't keep all her field guide notes in her head. She said them out loud to her teammates.

"When you're lost and camping," Tomoko said, "you look for different clues to help you find your way again. The sun can be a clue. Tracks can be clues. Weird rocks—or buildings—can be clues."

"People can be clues too," Kenzie said. "Right? Especially if you're camping in the city. Running into people is like running into an animal that can talk."

"Yeah," Bree said, "but sometimes animals are dangerous. You wouldn't ask a wolf or a bobcat for help."

Kenzie looked at Tomoko. "Is that how that lady was?"

Tomoko nodded. She wished people didn't always act like scary animals. She wished they would be helpful and nice all the time, the way Kenzie saw them.

The team turned another corner together.

"Hey, Tomonater!" Shelly called.

Tomoko turned around as Shelly bounced the basketball to her. Tomoko caught the ball and dribbled as she skated forward.

"Open!" Bree called.

Tomoko tossed the ball to Bree.

"Try a three-point pass to Kenzie!" Tomoko said.

"Got it, Coach!" Bree spun around and looped the basketball over her head toward Kenzie. Kenzie caught the ball. She bounced it over the pavement.

"Let's try a derby move," Jules said. "Kenzie can start off as jammer and then pass the ball to someone else in the pack!"

Tomoko smiled. "OK."

The Daredevils all gathered close together on the sidewalk in front of Kenzie. Kenzie rushed toward them, dribbling the ball as she skated.

"Jules!" Kenzie said. "Pass!"

She lobbed the ball at Jules, who caught it with one hand and skated forward.

"You guys are getting so good," Tomoko said. Her chest swelled with pride.

Jules laughed and skated toward the crosswalk.

"Hey!" Jules called. "I can see the convention center!"

Bree whooped and shook her hips. Both Shelly and Kenzie offered Tomoko fist bumps.

"The Tomonater's done it!" Kenzie said. "Time for the derby extravaganza!"

The line of girls rolled onto the crosswalk as the green WALK sign lit up. Jules was still holding Tomoko's basketball. She was trying to balance it on one finger.

"Don't mess with the ball while you're in the street," Bree said. "You'll lose it under a car."

"Yeah, yeah," Jules mumbled. The ball tilted in her hand. She swooped to catch it.

THUNK.

Tomoko and the others gasped as Jules sailed right into

a rain gutter along the other side of the road. Jules's knees buckled and she went down. The ball rolled up onto the sidewalk, nearly touching the front doors to the convention center.

"Jules!" Shelly cried.

They hurried over.

"Are you OK?" Kenzie asked.

"Ugh," Jules said. She groaned and rubbed her shin. "Why don't we have ankle guards in derby?"

"Probably because there are no gutters in derby," Bree said. She held out an arm. "Need help getting up?"

Jules took Bree's hand. She tried lifting her skate.

"I can't move it!" Jules said. She wiggled the wheel back and forth. It was trapped in the steel grating of the rain gutter. "I'm stuck."

Tomoko glanced at the WALK sign. The light would change soon and cars would start coming through . . . with Jules still planted on the side of the road.

"What should we do?" Shelly asked. Her voice wobbled.

Tomoko realized Shelly was looking at her.

The sun . . . the tracks . . . moving water . . .

None of Tomoko's field guide tips were coming in handy for a friend stuck in a sewer grate. She darted and looked around. Across the street, the same white lady was approaching the crosswalk. Tomoko winced.

Other hikers on the trail.

Kenzie was right. Other people could be resources sometimes. And Tomoko knew her teammates wouldn't leave her to deal with the woman on her own. Would they?

"Hey!" Tomoko waved her arms.

The woman frowned as she spotted the girls.

"I thought I said skating out here was a bad idea," she said as she approached the group. She narrowed her eyes at Tomoko.

Tomoko swallowed. She could feel her insides turning small.

Suddenly, Shelly stepped forward.

"We're trying to get back to our rink," Shelly said. "But our friend is stuck!"

Kenzie skated next to Shelly. She and Shelly stood protectively in front of Tomoko. Tomoko felt like the

jammer in the Daredevils' Madame President move,
where two blockers would safeguard the jammer through
the pack.

"We need help," Kenzie said to the woman. "Can you
make sure no cars run us over while we get Jules out?"

The woman looked taken aback. "No one's going to
run you over. And you really shouldn't be playing out in
the street."

"Like we said," Bree cut in, "we're just trying to get back to that building. Now are you going to help us or let us get hit by a car?"

The woman blinked at Bree. She turned to Jules, then Kenzie, then Shelly, then Tomoko. This time, Tomoko felt stronger when the woman looked at her. She knew that everyone was finally paying attention. It made her feel so much braver than she had been before, when she was all by herself.

"I'll help," the woman said feebly.

"Great." Bree turned and leaped onto the sidewalk. "I'm grabbing Mambo and the other coaches. We need some serious yanking to get that wheel out!"

Bree disappeared through the front doors. Tomoko and Shelly helped Jules sit back along the sidewalk curb. They yanked and tugged on Jules's skate, but it was still hopelessly stuck.

Kenzie and the woman waved their arms from the sidewalk to slow down the passing cars.

Tomoko sat on the curb next to Jules. She wiped her forehead.

"It won't budge," Tomoko said. "I think we need the coaches' help."

"That's OK," Jules said. She paused and looked at her foot. "Thanks for sticking by me."

Tomoko smiled. "That's what a team does," she said. She looked over at Kenzie, then Shelly, then back at Jules. "Thanks for sticking by me too."

CHAPTER SIXTEEN

THE CROSSWALK SIGN FLIPPED FROM *DON'T WALK* TO *WALK* three more times before the front doors to the convention center burst open. Mambo, Lo, and Bree all soared out.

"Over there!" Bree called. She pointed at the curb where Tomoko, Jules, and Shelly were sitting together. Kenzie and the older woman stood on either side of them.

"What in Jupiter—" Mambo wheeled over to Jules. "Are you hurt?" she asked breathlessly.

Jules shook her head. "Nope. I'm not sure about the skate, though."

Mambo knelt over the gutter grate. She unlaced Jules's skate and helped ease her foot out. "Next time, leave the skate behind, Crown Jules. It's not important."

"I'll say," the old woman sniffed. She lowered her arm and turned again down the sidewalk.

Lo caught up to the woman. "Thank you so much for looking after our kids," she said. "Pretty sure Bree Zee just gave us a heart attack when she said they were outside."

The woman shook her head.

"I was on my way to the store," she said. She tilted her chin at Tomoko. "This one nearly knocked me down."

"She did not!" Shelly said. She scrambled up to her skates. "We were all there!"

Lo held a hand flat toward Shelly.

"Cool it, Bomb Shell," Lo said quietly. She turned to the woman, her face a little sterner than it was before. "I can't imagine our Tomonater knocking anyone down outside of the derby track. But thank you for sticking by them until we got here."

"Humph!" The woman lifted her nose in the air and continued along the sidewalk.

Mambo and Lo traded a look with each other and shook their heads.

"Let's get this skate out of here," Mambo said. She grabbed the toe stop of Jules's skate while Lo grabbed the heel. They yanked one, two, three times until—*pop!*—the skate flew up in their hands.

Mambo brought the skate over to Jules. She tugged hard on the laces as she got Jules's foot back inside.

"Oof," Jules said. "You're tying it even tighter than I usually do!"

Mambo glanced at Jules. "I figure if I tie it tight enough, that might keep you from gallivanting off again!"

Jules's cheeks went red. She let Mambo help her up, then slunk over to Kenzie, Shelly, Tomoko, and Bree.

"Come on, Daredevils," Lo called. "Back inside before you start any other shenanigans."

The Daredevils shuffled between their two coaches. They passed under a giant clock hanging inside the convention center.

"Two oh four p.m.," Kenzie murmured to the others. "Guess we were gone longer than we thought."

Shelly shrugged. "The extravaganza's just starting. We're not that late."

"Correction," Lo said over her shoulder. "It *was* just starting. Everything got put on hold once we realized you never came back from your 'practice.'" She made her fingers into air quotes.

"It was a real derby practice!" Bree said. She hunched her shoulders. "We just ended up practicing somewhere else."

"Which you'll tell us all about in a hot minute," Mambo said. "Keep going."

The team ducked their heads as they followed Lo back through the labyrinth of halls toward the rink.

Lo opened the main doors.

The stands were filled with all the players from both the Austin and Dallas leagues. They stared, wide-eyed, as the Daredevils filed in.

"Uh-oh," someone called in a singsong voice. Tomoko didn't have to look around to know who it was.

"Oh brother," Bree said. She rolled her eyes and skated toward the stands.

"Nope," Mambo called. "This way."

Mambo signaled Bree and the rest of the team to the bunk area. Tomoko sighed as the Daredevils skated past both leagues. It felt like they were in a parade for roller derby delinquents.

Lo held the door open. Once Tomoko and Jules skated through last, she let the door close behind them. Mambo and Lo motioned the Daredevils toward their bunk corner.

The girls squeezed and sat together on Tomoko's and Kenzie's beds.

"All right," Mambo said. "Who's the ring leader of this operation?"

The Daredevils all looked at one another.

"That depends," Shelly said after a moment. "Do you mean, whose idea was it to leave the rink in the first place?"

"That'd be me," Bree said, raising her hand.

"OK," Mambo said. "Well—"

"But if you mean who got us all lost? That'd be us." Shelly raised her hand along with Jules and Kenzie.

Lo raised her eyebrows. "Kenzilla?"

Kenzie blushed and nodded. She dropped her hand on her lap.

Mambo turned to Tomoko. "So everyone's the ring leader but the Tomonater?"

"No," Bree said. "The Tomonater was the actual leader. She got us back using all her nature skills!"

"Yeah," Jules added, "and then when I got my skate stuck, she flagged that lady down to help us, even though the lady had been totally mean to her earlier."

"Mean how?" Mambo asked. Her eyebrows were furrowed. "Did someone hurt you?"

Tomoko shook her head. "No," she mumbled.

"It was a *microaggression*," Kenzie said, stringing the word out slowly. "The lady was being mean about Tomoko's size."

"I see."

Mambo tapped her chin. She looked over at Lo. "Well, what we really want to know is why y'all felt like you needed to leave in the first place. We wanted to have a great week of roller derby—especially on our last day! What made you decide to take off?"

"Microaggressions," Bree muttered.

"What now?" Lo asked. She turned to Bree, then to Tomoko. "Tomonater, fill us in. What happened?"

Tomoko sighed. "Bree had the idea to have a Daredevils practice on a basketball court so we could use my ball," she said. "She was being nice because this week hasn't been . . . well, it wasn't exactly . . ."

Mambo's expression softened. "Wasn't exactly what?"

Tomoko's chest tightened. "I just felt really alone," she said. "One of the Dallas players kept saying things."

"Tomonater." Lo squatted in front of the bed across from Tomoko. "You can always tell us if someone else makes you feel uncomfortable. You *should* always tell us. There's no room for that in roller derby."

Tomoko held her cheeks in her hands.

"That's not on you," Mambo said. "If someone says something nasty, that shows a lot more about them than anyone else."

"Who was it?" Lo asked.

Tomoko glanced at her teammates. Shelly and Kenzie nodded.

"Her name's Emma," Tomoko whispered.

Lo stood up and nodded at Mambo. She skated back out the door. For a moment, Tomoko was scared about what would happen. Then she remembered how good it felt when all the Daredevils stood up with her to the older woman. It felt good to have the coaches on her side too.

Mambo looked back and forth between the teammates. "I'm definitely not happy about your choices today," she said. "But I'm glad y'all stuck up for each other. Next time, just tell us when something's bugging you on or off the track. And for Pete's sake—don't give us the slip again! Deal?"

"Deal!" the Daredevils said together.

Mambo gave the girls a tight smile. "All right then," she said. She clapped her hands. "Let's get to the extravaganza!"

CHAPTER SEVENTEEN

ALL THE TEAMS WERE DRESSED IN THEIR OFFICIAL uniforms for the extravaganza.

The Daredevils carefully unpacked a rainbow of sequined accessories from their bags. Shelly had designed the uniforms for their tournament in the spring. Each of the Daredevils got to wear a different color.

Tomoko slipped on her red sequined sleeves and placed her Tomonater red robot buttons on her knee pads. She led her sparkly team out of the bunks and back into the main rink. The rest of the players were still there. All but one person.

"Where's Emma?" Bree whispered.

Tomoko shrugged. She noticed that Lo and one of the Dallas league coaches weren't around either.

Mambo placed her whistle in her mouth.

Fffttt!

"Derby teams, to the track!"

Derby players dressed as outlaws, zombies, and even ravenous barracuda fish rolled into the rink.

"Nice sequins," a Dallas barracuda said to Tomoko.

"Thanks," Tomoko said.

She lined up between her teammates. The coaches helped all the players spread out over the track. Mambo blew the whistle again and they started off doing the same kind of drills they had been working on all week.

"Pushcarts! Grab a partner from the other league!" a Dallas coach called.

Tomoko twisted her head around. Emma was still out with Lo. But another Dallas player was skating toward Tomoko.

"You got a partner yet?" the girl asked. She was dressed in an orange-and-blue uniform, with a flame painted on one cheek and an ice crystal painted on the other.

Tomoko shook her head.

"Awesome!" the girl said. "I'm Renee, but my derby name is the Renee-gade."

"I'm Tomoko," Tomoko said. "My derby name is the Tomonater."

"Like the killer robot!" Renee grinned. "Hey! Our names sort of make a little team. *The* Renee-gade. *The* Tomonater. Get it?"

"The '*The*' team," Tomoko said.

Renee laughed. "Exactly!"

Tomoko and Renee decided to have Renee push first.

This time, when the whistle blew, Tomoko didn't feel scary hands jabbing into her back. Renee pushed her smoothly over the track while Tomoko steered by angling her skates. Then they switched places and Tomoko pressed into Renee's back around the rink.

The The team stuck together for the next set of exercises. Renee and Tomoko practiced hip checks on each other. They raced in loops together.

"What do you like to do outside of derby?" Renee asked as they set up for a crossover drill. "My older brother's teaching me how to knit!"

"Cool," Tomoko said. "I like to go camping with my uncle. I actually thought this was going to be more like a derby camping trip." Her cheeks flushed a little.

"I saw your hiking backpack," Renee said. She smiled. "It would be so cool to combine derby camp with camping!"

The heat in Tomoko's cheeks trickled down into her chest. She smiled back at Renee.

"I also play basketball," she said. "Actually, my team sort of invented this derby basketball game so we could play on skates."

Renee's eyes lit up. "Oh! I want to try it! The Fire and Icies would be so into derby basketball!"

The two girls went through the last of the drills together, trading tips about knitting patterns for skate-covers and how to dribble a basketball while wearing wrist guards. Tomoko glanced at the other Daredevils hanging out and laughing with Dallas players. Now she finally got why they were so excited to talk about their partners each night. Making new friends could be awesome.

Mambo blew the whistle again.

"Time to rejoin your teams!" she called. "We're going to have a set of scrimmages against each other, then play some games!"

Tomoko fist-bumped Renee, then skated back to the other Daredevils.

"Was your partner cool?" Bree asked as Tomoko rolled over.

Tomoko grinned and nodded. "Yep! Really cool!"

The Daredevils watched two other teams get called onto the track for the first scrimmage: The Austin Cow Pokes were up against the Dallas Fire & Icies.

"Go Cow Pokes! Go Fire and Icies!" Tomoko shouted.

From the corner of her eye, Tomoko saw Lo wave her over to the snack bar. Emma was by her side.

Tomoko took a deep breath. Her stomach flopped. She got up from the stands.

Shelly turned her head. "Want us to come?" she asked.

"No thanks," Tomoko said. "I think I need to do this for myself."

"OK," Kenzie said. She glanced at Lo in the corner. "Just call us if you need us."

"Thanks, Kenzilla," Tomoko said. She turned and skated around the edge of the rink.

Lo, Emma, and the Dallas coach were waiting for her.

Tomoko felt her palms go cold and clammy. She couldn't help worrying that somehow, she was the one in trouble. She tried to shake the feeling away.

"Come have a seat," Lo said, motioning to one of the tables.

Tomoko sat next to Lo, directly across from Emma. Lo tilted her head toward Emma.

"Want to get us started?" Lo asked.

Emma's lips were pressed tight. Her eyes were squinty, and Tomoko noticed that she kept flicking her gaze back and forth between the track and the table.

"Sorry for saying those things earlier," Emma muttered. She scratched her nail over the tabletop.

The Dallas coach placed a hand on Emma's shoulder. "Let's get a bit more specific," she said, "so Tomoko knows that you've really had some time to consider how important it is to be kind, open, and inclusive in roller derby."

"Yeah," Emma said. She was still muttering. "Sorry about the thing I said about kimchi. Also about your backpack. Also about, you know—"

She motioned to Tomoko.

"You."

Lo sighed through her nostrils. She laced her fingers together. "That it?"

"Uh-huh," Emma said.

Tomoko's leg bounced up and down. She wanted to get out of there as fast as she could. Even with the coaches beside her, somehow Emma still made Tomoko feel like the opposite of the Tomonater.

Tomoko knew how these kinds of talks with grown-ups went. *It's fine,* she could say. Then she'd be able to get up and go back to her team.

But Tomoko thought about her camping field guide again. She thought about how it helped her be a leader before, out in the maze of downtown. Maybe it could help her be a leader here too. She flipped through the pages in her mind.

- When acting as a guide for others, it's important for a hiker to remain brave even when temporarily disoriented.

Tomoko swallowed. She remembered the rest of that page's advice.

- Bravery, of course, doesn't mean the hiker is not afraid. It means they keep a cool head despite their fear.

Tomoko mentally closed the book and set it aside. She raised her chin and looked directly across the table at Emma. "Why did you want to make me feel bad?" Tomoko asked.

Emma's eyes widened in surprise. She shrugged, her own shoulders hunching inward.

"I don't know," she said quietly.

Tomoko placed her arms on the table. She leaned forward. "Well, I'm proud of all the things that make me, me. I like my hiking backpack. I like my size. I like that my mom and uncle were born in Japan because it makes me feel closer to my culture."

Emma's shoulders scrunched up the whole time Tomoko

spoke. Meanwhile, Tomoko felt her spine stretch as she sat up taller.

"Being different isn't a bad thing," Tomoko said. "It's actually really awesome. If people are confused about me, I'd rather they ask good questions instead of saying hurtful things."

"Well said, Tomoko." Lo nudged Tomoko's elbow. She looked at the Dallas coach. "Maybe Emma can continue thinking about that advice, as well as her actions, on the bench this afternoon."

Emma's face fell.

Tomoko studied Emma for a moment. She turned to Lo.

"She can also learn about some different derby moves on the track," Tomoko said. "The Daredevils have a fun game we wanted to show everyone."

Lo smiled at Tomoko. She paused, then turned to Emma.

"Does that sound like something you want to learn about respectfully?"

Emma bobbed her head. She pushed herself up from the table. Both Tomoko and Emma skated toward the stands.

"Thanks," Emma said as she skated next to Tomoko.

But before Tomoko could say anything back, Jules reached over and squeezed Tomoko's hand.

"The Daredevils are up for our scrimmage," Jules said. She pulled Tomoko onto the track behind her.

Tomoko settled behind the blocker line with Kenzie, Jules, and Shelly. Kenzie and Shelly looked toward the stands at Emma, then back to Tomoko.

"Everything good?" Kenzie asked.

Tomoko smiled and gave a thumbs-up.

CHAPTER EIGHTEEN

TOMOKO PUT ALL THE NEW THINGS SHE HAD LEARNED during derby camp into practice as the Austin Daredevils scrimmaged against the Dallas Barracudas.

Tomoko knew how to duck out of the way just in time if a blocker tried to hip check her. She knew how to squeeze between blockers to get to the jammer.

Thanks to the Daredevils' secret practice, Tomoko even knew how to catch the jammer star panty when Bree passed it to her mid jam.

"The Tomonater is killing it!" someone called from the stands.

Tomoko grinned at Renee as she zipped around the track.

The Daredevils won their scrimmage, then watched from the sides as the next several scrimmages unfolded.

The Dallas coaches called the score of the final scrimmage. Tomoko and the others cheered as the two teams streamed off the rink and shuffled into the stands.

"You've all improved so much!" Raz said. "I wish we could do derby camp every week!"

"Now for the real fun," Lo said, standing next to Raz. She rubbed her hands together deviously. "Who's up for some derby games?"

Tomoko whooped along with her teammates. The coaches separated the big group of players into two halves. Tomoko and the other Daredevils took to the track in the first group as they geared up to play tag, then leapfrog, then a round of red light/green light.

"Green light!" a Dallas coach yelled out.

The players raced forward.

"Red light!" the coach suddenly said, holding her palm flat.

Bree turned to Tomoko. "This feels sort of familiar," she said.

Tomoko laughed. The coach's hand did remind her a little of all the red hands at the crosswalk signs that day. But overall, getting lost in the city felt like it had happened so long ago. It was a small memory in Tomoko's head, like standing on top of a tall mountain and looking at the tiny campsite below. Being lost was behind them now. Tomoko could see ahead for miles.

The Renee-gade was in Tomoko's group for playing games. Tomoko offered Renee a fist bump whenever they passed by each other.

"OK groups, switch it up!" Mambo called.

Fffttt!

"Hey," Renee said when they were all off the track. She skated over to Tomoko and the Daredevils. "I told the Fire and Icies about your derby basketball game and they all want to learn! Can we play?"

Several other Fire & Icies players gathered next to Renee.

"This is the Tomonater? Hi!" one player said.

"I love basketball, but I never made the school team," another girl said.

Kenzie's head popped up next to Tomoko's shoulder.

"Derby basketball's way better than regular basketball anyway," Kenzie said, smiling.

One of the Fire & Icies pointed to the main doors. "There's a basketball court down the hall!" she said. "I'll bet the coaches would let us go use it!"

Shelly's cheeks went red. "Oh. We already tried that this morning . . . it didn't go so well."

"We heard," the Fire & Icies player said, laughing. "Y'all had a big adventure downtown! But I bet if one of the Dallas coaches went with us, they'd say it was OK. I'll ask this time."

The player turned and skated toward Lo and another Dallas coach standing off of the track. Lo listened carefully to the player, then looked across the rink at the Daredevils.

"Pleeeeaaase?" Jules called out. She pressed her palms together. "We won't go anywhere!"

The Dallas coach whispered something in Lo's ear. Both coaches nodded at each other, then skated toward the group.

"We'll take you if the rest of this half wants to play," Lo said.

The Fire & Icies pumped their fists in the air. "Yes! They totally will! Who wouldn't want to learn derby basketball?"

While the Fire & Icies and Daredevils spread the word about the derby basketball game, Tomoko grabbed her basketball from where she had left it on her bunk. She glanced at her hiking backpack peeking out from under her bed and smiled.

"I've got it!" Tomoko said as she emerged from the bunks.

The rest of the group—both Dallas and Austin players—were waiting by the doors. They skated in twos down the hall, chatting with each other about the rest of their summers and what the fall bout season would be like. Tomoko hoped they would get to play the Dallas league sometime again soon.

As the group swept into the indoor basketball court, everyone spread out between the two nets, then turned expectantly toward Tomoko.

Tomoko took a deep breath.

"Derby basketball's a lot like regular basketball," she said.

"Except the person with the ball is sort of like the jammer. Everyone's trying to hip check them and grab the ball, but only one person from each team can actually score."

"That's awesome!" one of the Dallas players said. "Do we play like the scrimmages? Two teams at a time?"

"Sure," Tomoko said. She bounced the ball to Renee. "The Fire and Icies can start against the Barracudas."

Renee caught the ball in both hands. She glanced at Tomoko.

"I'm probably not very good," Renee said quietly. Tomoko could tell that she was nervous.

"Don't worry," Tomoko said. "I'll be here to help." She skated over to the side of the court.

"Just try dribbling the ball and skating forward," Tomoko said. "You really have to lean into it, but the ball will catch you."

Renee hunched over and bounced the ball. She shifted her skates.

"You've got it!" Tomoko said.

She skated between the grown-up coaches as she watched the two teams go head-to-head on the court. Tomoko helped to signal when the ball went out of bounds or when one of the players was traveling. By the end of the scrimmage, both teams had gotten the hang of derby basketball.

"Nice job out there!" Lo said. She looked down at Tomoko and winked. "Nice job to you too, Coach."

Tomoko blushed and smiled. She grabbed the ball and sailed onto the court as the Daredevils showed off their new moves in front of the other teams.

Once everyone had gotten a chance to play, the derby players all formed a big circle in the middle of the court. They passed the basketball around and around to one another, making up games of their own.

A Dallas player turned to the Daredevils.

"Someone from Austin told me you ran away from people chasing you." She bounced the ball to Jules. "That true?"

Jules caught the ball and turned to the others.

"Umm . . ."

"It's not really true," Bree said. "We thought a guy was going to call the coaches on us. But we didn't actually see anyone after us."

"We just got really, really lost," Kenzie said. "Dallas is way different from Austin."

Some of the Dallas players laughed.

"I bet Austin's way different from Dallas," one of them said.

"But the Tomonater got us out," Shelly piped up. She beamed at Tomoko. "She used her wilderness skills to track the sun and shadows and stuff!"

One of the Fire & Icies clapped. "Nice going, Wilderness Girl!"

Tomoko's skin went cold for a moment. She remembered what it had felt like when Emma had called her Wilderness Girl as she first stepped into the rink with her hiking backpack. She blinked and looked up. Renee was looking back at her.

"You said you knew how to camp!" Renee said. "I guess you figured out how to combine it with derby after all!"

Warmth *whooshed* back into Tomoko's chest.

"Yeah," Tomoko said. She smiled. "I guess I did."

Suddenly, all the players wanted to hear about how the Daredevils got lost in the city and how they made their way back out again. Tomoko tucked her basketball under her arm and found a seat on the stands next to the basketball court. Everyone gathered close around her.

Tomoko cleared her throat.

She could almost smell the campfire and roasting marsh-mallows as she began to tell the story of how the Daredevils made their way out of the urban forest.

ACKNOWLEDGMENTS

It's easy to get lost along the long and windy trail of publishing. Luckily, I'm hiking beside three of the most brilliant and courageous people in the business. Courtney Code, Lauren Spieller, and Sophie Escabasse—thank you thank you thank you. You three have been this series' compass.

There's no team I'd rather trek with than the fine people at Amulet and Abrams. Thank you all so much for your hard work and unwavering support. Special thanks to Marcie Lawrence for keeping the team in style and to Mary Marolla and Jenny Choy for finding connections at every turn.

Climbing new mountains is a scary thing, but having the expertise and advice of Sachiko Burton at Salt & Sage Books has made even the steepest stretch feel possible. Thank you, Sachiko, for shedding so much light on Tomoko's story. Any issues that remain are my sole responsibility, and I am listening and learning constantly.

Motherhood has complicated my writing in a way I never could have anticipated. Loriel Ryon, Jennifer Sigler, and Holly Chamblee—you've been my post markers down this very particular path. Thank you. I love each of you.

Jim, Cymeon, and Brooke Watters, thank you for first setting me toward the way of adventure, of the unknown, of dreams peeking between the branches. David Rosewater, thank you for clearing the bramble and pushing me forward.

August Rosewater, thank you for listening to all my campfire stories. Prepare for a lifetime of this, kiddo.

ABOUT THE AUTHOR

Kit Rosewater writes books for children. Before she was an author, Kit taught theater to middle school students, which even a world-renowned cat herder once called "a lot of work." Kit has a master's degree in children's literature. She lives in Albuquerque, New Mexico, with her adoring spouse, her adorable baby, and a border collie who takes up most of the bed. *The Derby Daredevils: Tomoko Takes the Lead* is the third book in Kit's Derby Daredevils series. Catch her online at kitrosewater.com or @kitrosewater.

ABOUT THE ILLUSTRATOR

Sophie Escabasse is the author-illustrator of the graphic novel *The Witches of Brooklyn*. She lives in Brooklyn, New York, with her family. Find her online at esofii.com or @esofiii.